PRAISE FOR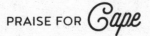

"Readers across genres will be enamored by this blend of history, mystery, and superpowered action." —*Booklist*, starred review

"Hannigan takes on history, prejudice, friendship, and bravery with aplomb. Fans of fast-paced action adventures, computer science, and confident main characters will enjoy this series debut that is sure to fly off the shelves." —*SLJ*

"With interwoven action sequences told in comics panels, the tale has the exciting pace of a superhero adventure. Puzzles readers can solve are the icing on this cake." —*Kirkus Reviews*

"*Cape* is a book with something for everyone—codes to crack, villains to vanquish, and a trio of superheroes who just might save the world. An absolutely original story, filled with so much excitement that the pages practically turn themselves." —Frances O'Roark Dowell, Edgar Award–winning author of *Dovey Coe*

"A one-two punch of heroism and fun!" —Ingrid Law, Newbery Honor winner and *New York Times* bestselling author of *Savvy*

"Josie, Mae, and Akiko aren't just the friends and superheroes we need today; they're the friends and superheroes we need to *be* today. These girls rock!" —Liesl Shurtliff, *New York Times* bestselling author of the *Time Castaways* trilogy

"Kate Hannigan does more than write a rip-roaring girls' adventure story. She brings back to life real women who were real superheroines . . . along with some sadly forgotten but wonderful fictional superheroines who predated Wonder Woman. I can't wait for book two!" —Trina Robbins, author of *Babes in Arms, Women in Comics During the Second World War*

Don't miss the other adventures in
THE LEAGUE OF SECRET HEROES series!

Cape

Coming soon

Boots

THE LEAGUE OF SECRET HEROES

Mask

Book Two

By KATE HANNIGAN

Illustrated by PATRICK SPAZIANTE

Aladdin

New York London Toronto Sydney New Delhi

ALADDIN

An imprint of Simon & Schuster Children's Publishing Division

1230 Avenue of the Americas, New York, New York 10020

First Aladdin hardcover edition August 2020

For information about special discounts for bulk purchases, please contact Simon & Schuster Special Sales at 1-866-506-1949 or business@simonandschuster.com.

The Simon & Schuster Speakers Bureau can bring authors to your live event. For more information or to book an event contact the Simon & Schuster Speakers Bureau at 1-866-248-3049 or visit our website at www.simonspeakers.com.

Series design by Sammy Yuen Jr.

Book design by Laura Lyn DiSiena

The illustrations for this book were rendered digitally.

The text of this book was set in Marion.

Manufactured in the United States of America 0720 BVG

2 4 6 8 10 9 7 5 3 1

Library of Congress Cataloging-in-Publication Data

Names: Hannigan, Kate, author. | Spaziante, Patrick, illustrator.

Title: Mask / by Kate Hannigan ; illustrated by Patrick Spaziante.

Description: First Aladdin hardcover edition. | New York : Aladdin, 2020. | Series: The League of Secret Heroes ; book 2 | Audience: Ages 8-12. | Summary: Akiko, Mae, and Josie, also called the Infinity Trinity, spring into action after learning that a spy is betraying secrets to the Japanese military--and that Akiko's mother may be involved.

Identifiers: LCCN 2020018906 (print) | LCCN 2020018907 (ebook) | ISBN 9781534439146 (hardcover) | ISBN 9781534439160 (ebook)

Subjects: CYAC: Superheroes—Fiction. | Spies—Fiction. | Ciphers—Fiction. | Japanese Americans—Fiction. | World War, 1939-1945—United States—Fiction.

Classification: LCC PZ7.H198158 Mas 2020 (print) | LCC PZ7.H198158 (ebook) | DDC [Fic]—dc23

LC record available at https://lccn.loc.gov/2020018906

For the Usual Suspects

Manzanar.

Two

$\mathcal{Y}$OU CAN TALK ABOUT THINGS ALL YOU LIKE. But what really matters is taking that first step toward actually *doing* something.

Or in our case, I guess it's more like taking that first leap—into the air and flying.

After battling the serpentlike Hisser and stopping the Duke and his band of Nazi spies, we had been feeling pretty good. Not only had Akiko, Mae, and I kept my cousin Kay and the other Secret Six computer programmers safe, we'd also kept the ENIAC—that blinking heap of metal Kay and Jean had called a giant electronic brain—from falling into the wrong hands.

But the next morning, after Mrs. B had stood up from our booth at Gerda's Diner and left us, things got a little more complicated. That was when our puzzling skills had really kicked in. We'd figured out that Mrs. B and Astra weren't just members of the league of secret heroes. They were superheroes themselves—the Palomino and her wolfy sidekick, Star!

There have been others taken by villains, she'd told us. *Many others.*

And this is where you come in.

It was clear to me that Mrs. B wasn't expecting the Infinity Trinity just to fly around Philadelphia rescuing cats from trees or slowing down the occasional runaway train. She had big plans. As in saving her sister, Zenobia, who happened to be the most important superhero of all time.

"We're going to need to practice our superpowers for a few hours every day," Akiko was saying as she poked her straw around her milkshake. "And keep our superhero costumes clean," added Mae, who was the tidiest person I'd ever met.

"And what should we call Mrs. B and Astra now? Mrs. Palomino? Mr. Star?"

That was Mae again. Tidy and polite, even to a dog.

Their ideas kept piling up, one after another. But for me, my mind was stuck like one of those kiddie rides at the amusement park—the kind that go around and around but never get anywhere. I kept thinking the same thing: Zenobia was in danger. And she didn't just need help. She needed *our* help. As in the three of us. Akiko Nakano, Mae Crumpler, and me, Josie Mary Maeve O'Malley.

One asthmatic know-it-all.

One animal-obsessed know-it-all. And—

"Are you listening, Josie?" Akiko's gravelly voice interrupted my thoughts. I dropped my fork. "You might think you know everything about superheroes and, well, life. But it's time you listen to Mae and me."

"And you should consider wearing a broad-brimmed hat," added Mae, sipping her chocolate malted and gesturing toward my face. "You're pretty pink today."

My hands automatically shot up to my freckled cheeks. I guess it was clear what they thought of me: I was a sunburned know-it-all.

"Why don't you take charge for a while, Akiko?" I asked, hoping my voice sounded light and not as worried as I was feeling. "I'm fine listening to you and Mae."

"All I'm saying is that if Mrs. B calls on the Infinity Trinity this summer," Akiko said, plowing ahead in that sandpaper voice of hers, "you can't be stuck babysitting your little brothers."

"She's right," agreed Mae. "Granny Crumpler is going to want me helping her open the new library branch. But I cannot possibly stack mysteries on shelves when I could be out solving them!" And then she leaned in and whispered, "In a superhero costume, too!"

Before I could reply, Mae and Akiko steamrolled ahead like they were flattening tar onto a new road. "We can have Mrs. B send a letter to our families so they don't worry about where we are," said Mae. "We'll tell them we're going to sleepaway camp or somewhere," said Akiko.

I opened my mouth to speak. But they kept on rolling. "We need to make a list of what superheroes have been spotted and where." That was Akiko. She pulled a pencil and notebook out of her Hauntima bag and began taking notes. "And what was happening when any superheroes went missing," added Mae, tapping the page and urging Akiko to write faster. "Were they vaporized like the Stretcher? Were they stunned? frozen? turned invisible?"

I took another bite of my blueberry pie as Akiko and Mae added to their list. Their banter became background noise to the voice in my head. I kept coming back to the same thought as before:

Zenobia was legendary. Zenobia was the most beloved superhero of all time. Zenobia was the type of hero memorialized in statues and street names and songs! She was powerful, smart, clever, inventive. In a word, she was everything.

So how exactly were three kids like us supposed to save her?

It went on like this for nearly a week—until Wednesday. That's the day we took off for San Francisco.

But it wasn't like we just packed our suitcases and climbed aboard a train from Philadelphia, the way most people travel. Things with the three of us, I was quickly learning, weren't exactly typical anymore.

"Could we please find somewhere to cool off?" I had been asking this question for nearly an hour. It wasn't even ten in the morning, and already I'd felt my shirt sticking to my back. "I can't stand this heat."

"Let's go to my aunt and uncle's store," Akiko had suggested. "A fire hydrant burst, and it's been gushing water like a fountain for the past two days. We won't even need to change into bathing suits."

This had sounded good to Mae and me, so we started walking. But as soon as we'd turned onto Akiko's block, one of her cousins had come running toward us. He'd waved an envelope in his hand and practically knocked her over trying to give it to her.

"For me?" Akiko'd said, steadying her little cousin. He looked to be about the same age as Baby Lou, though he had both his front teeth. "Why's it already opened if it's for me?"

"I didn't mean to read it," he'd confessed. "I thought it might have baseball cards inside. I'm looking for Joe DiMaggio and Yogi Berra cards, see, so I can trade 'em with—"

"So you tore into my mail?" interrupted Akiko. "I'm pretty sure opening somebody's mail is against the law, Squirt."

I'd tried not to smile. Hearing Akiko, who weighed about as much as a baseball card, refer to her little cousin as "Squirt" made me want to laugh. Mae had shifted her feet, and I could tell she was hiding a smile too. All three of us were just as scrawny as this little guy.

"But it's really important," Squirt had insisted, his voice growing louder. "It's about your mom, Akiko. I read it three times. The letter says she's gone missing!"

Three

ANDND THAT'S HOW WE WOUND UP ON THE West Coast, flying around California.

"Manzanar?" Mae whispered.

"I'm sorry if I sound like a lunkhead, Akiko," I began, hoping she wouldn't say that she already *knew* I was a lunkhead. "But I just don't understand how a whole neighborhood of people could get moved out into the desert like that."

"It wasn't just my block in Japantown that got moved, Josie. It was the whole community. And not only here in San Francisco, but in all of the cities in California—from Los Angeles and San Diego in the south, straight up the coast."

She reached up to adjust the barrette in her hair, like she needed something to do with her nervous energy.

"Japanese Americans were ordered out of Oregon and Washington too," she added. "Out of the whole West Coast."

"Everybody to the same camp?" whispered Mae.

"No. The government has set up lots of them—ten altogether. There's a couple east of here in California. And the rest are in Arizona, Utah, Idaho, Wyoming, Colorado, and even over in Arkansas."

Mae and I went quiet. Akiko already told us that grandparents and little kids were forced to relocate to the camps, right along with the grown men and women. I tried to imagine Baby Lou and Vinnie leaving our apartment for the desert.

"Hauntima's ghost! There's a copper," Akiko said, and I knew she was trying to whisper. I watched a black-and-white police car slow down at the corner behind us. "I can't get caught here in Japantown."

We shuffled closer toward a shrub blooming with flowers of the brightest pink I'd ever seen. Out of sight from the street, the three of us leaned in tightly together and grabbed each other's right hands.

"I know how the two of you are—you have to see something to believe it," said Akiko. "And I don't blame you, since I'm the same way."

As we straightened up, shoulder to shoulder in the triangle formed by our three bodies, I felt the familiar hum of electricity begin to pulse in my ears. What a week ago had seemed unbelievable was now just part of who we were. Golden light shot skyward and enveloped us in a churning funnel—like we were in the center of a hurricane. Swirls of purple, orange, and green danced before my eyes as our hair whipped in all directions.

Then we were off the ground, hanging suspended just a few feet above the sidewalk as the force of our transformation lifted us. Seconds after, we dropped back to the ground, and I heard Akiko's voice. I knew she was calling out our destination.

With that familiar *Pop!* my stomach dropped and we were teleporting again.

Just as the first time—when I appeared in Toby Hunter's apartment with an armload of his stolen bikes—the same dizzying feeling rushed over me. It was like we were plunging down an elevator shaft, and my stomach lurched up into my throat. If I weren't so nervous about what we'd see at the other end, it might have been fun.

I heard the *Pop!* again as we appeared on a hot and dusty patch of land, though I wasn't sure exactly where. I knew it must have been the internment camp Akiko had described, but I didn't really know what that meant.

Ah-choo!

"Allergies here too," Akiko complained, rubbing at her nose with an orange-gloved hand. "Never mind. Follow me."

In the blink of a dry and scratchy eye, we transformed back into our regular clothes. But my stomach kept right on dropping. I was worrying about how we'd explain ourselves to anyone who asked what we were doing here. Akiko had mentioned barbed wire and towers with guns. It took me only a few quick glances around to spot them.

I shoved my hands into the pockets of my dungarees to keep Akiko and Mae from noticing how much they were shaking. Mam's voice echoed in my head: *Be safe. No trouble.* I listened for footsteps, certain that at any minute an armed guard was going to grab us by the shoulders. How would I explain any of this to my mother?

"Josie, close your mouth," whispered Mae. "You're breathing as loud as Akiko."

"Okay, but I'm just a little nervous!" I tried speaking as softly as I could, but this was serious. "What are we going to say when someone catches us?"

"She's right," agreed Mae, tugging on Akiko's arm. "Neither one of us looks like you. What happens if somebody asks us what we're doing here?"

We began walking under the blazing sun, following a dusty path that seemed to divide rows of long wooden buildings. The sky was a cloudless blue, and waves of hot air rose off the rocks and dirt beneath us like the heat beams Zenobia could shoot from her eyes. Laundry hung on clotheslines, and little kids were playing catch and jumping rope.

As far as I could see ahead of us and behind, these same buildings repeated on and on and on. Far in the distance stood snow-capped mountains.

"This is Manzanar," Akiko said. She was clearly trying to speak quietly. I glanced left and right to see if anyone had noticed us. Akiko went on talking.

"Like I said before, this place is in the desert, though I'm not exactly sure where," she explained. "Still in California, I think. I've read about the death camps in Europe that the Nazis run—this isn't like that. But still, all of us are packed in here, and there's no privacy for sleeping or eating or showering. Or even using the bathroom.

"Everybody here is a prisoner."

Mae started in, doing that thing where she asks lots of questions—about the food and going to school and what they did to pass the time. But I had only one thing on my mind.

"What do we say?" I asked. "When a guard comes? We're not supposed to be here, Akiko!" I was practically shouting now. "Mam doesn't want any trouble!"

"We'll say you're visiting my troop." Akiko shrugged in a matter-of-fact way. "I'm a Girl Scout, and sometimes we invite other Scout troops from the nearby towns to come visit, work on badges together, that sort of thing. The Boy Scouts do it too."

Akiko didn't seem as panicky as me, so I tried to steady my breathing. Sometimes worrying seemed to be my true superpower. But Mae must have been thinking about trouble too, because her eyes were stuck on a nearby gun tower. She asked Akiko to do all the talking if anyone approached.

"So many people," I whispered, stumbling as I tried to keep up with Mae and Akiko. Off to the left of our dusty path, a lizard froze like a statue. It was about the size of my shoe, and its eyes moved like searchlights in all directions as it studied us. Lifting my gaze, I saw clusters of teenagers, grown-ups, white-haired grandparents, noisy little kids. The camp was like its own city.

Despite the drab sameness of the clapboard barracks, Akiko knew her way around. She turned us down a sort of alley between buildings, and then down another. Close to ten thousand people were living at Manzanar, she told us.

"Up ahead is where the camp choir practices," she announced with a nod, finally coming to a stop in front of another long, plain building. "Behind us, where we began, is where families live. But over here is where school happens, where clubs meet, and where we eat all our meals."

Each building looked the same as the next.

"There's a choir?" Mae asked. "And clubs?"

"We make the best of a terrible situation. We're prisoners—what else are we supposed to do all day?"

I heard singing and turned to study Akiko's face. Her expression was somewhere between angry and sad. The voices floated out of the building like puffs of cottonwood and rose in the hot, dusty air.

I shuddered thinking about Akiko and her family being stuck here instead of living in their old neighborhood back in San Francisco. When we were in Japantown, she'd taken us past not only the toy store where she'd bought her comic books, but also her church where she'd sung in the choir on Sundays, her school, and where her Girl Scout troop held its meetings. Now all of that happened here, behind barbed wire.

"My mom never misses choir practice," Akiko said. "We'll make sure she's there, and then we can get going. That letter my cousin gave me must have been a mistake."

She grabbed our hands and pulled us down a pathway in between another two barracks. We slinked along the length of the building until we were about halfway down, partly tiptoeing, partly tripping over the rocky ground. Akiko kept telling us to hush, but nobody could compare to her noisy breathing.

Without saying a word, she signaled for us to lock our fingers and make a foothold for her to stand in. Then she leaned against our shoulders and stepped into our cupped hands. "Okay, now stand up straighter," she croaked, digging a knee into my shoulder. "I can almost see inside the window!"

Lucky for us, Akiko was a good climber.

But not so lucky for us, she was allergic to pretty much everything. Especially dusty, dirt-covered buildings.

*A*H-CHOO!

"Get her!"

Mae and I were struggling to keep Akiko lifted to the window when three figures suddenly came running toward us from the top of the alley. My knees turned to spaghetti and my hands went weak. Just before we dropped Akiko completely, she jumped to the ground.

"What are you doing here, Akiko?" squealed a boy who must have been about five or six. "Is Tommy with you? I want to see him wearing his army uniform."

Two girls about the same size as the boy rushed to hug Akiko, wrapping their arms around her waist and pressing their faces into her faded dress. Then, as if one body, they began shuffling their feet, moving like a six-legged lizard toward the front of the barracks. When the boy decided to wrap his arms around Akiko too, it made for an eight-legged, shuffling desert octopus.

Akiko laughed and hugged them back, tousling their hair and patting their shoulders. I was stunned and at the same time relieved. We had been caught, but we didn't seem to be in trouble.

Yet.

Mae shook her head beside me and whispered, "I've never seen Akiko so . . ." She was searching for the right word. And so was I. *Pleasant? Not cranky? Un-irritable?*

"Nice," Mae finally said, sounding a little surprised. "She won't show an ounce of affection to dogs. But kinder-gartners seem to be another story. Look at her!"

"If she had two knucklehead brothers the way I do," I whispered back, "then I bet she'd come around to puppies."

Akiko stopped before her group hug reached the end of our alley. We watched as she dropped to one knee and looked her young friends in the eye. She was talking softly, holding their hands and leaning in close. Mae and I hung back to give them privacy.

After a few minutes, the kids scampered off.

"They haven't seen my mom for a long time," she said. Her fingers fiddled with the strap of her Hauntima bag.

"You know how little kids are," Mae said gently. "A long time for them might mean ten minutes."

"Maybe they're mixing up your mom with someone else," I suggested. "Maybe they're not remembering right."

But Akiko was firm. She gazed up at Mae and me, then let out a long breath.

"No. My mom sings in the choir, and she teaches the little ones too. These kids love her. They're not confused."

But I was. Where could her mom have gone? Akiko had been granted permission to leave, for farmwork, she'd told us. So long as she stayed far away from the West Coast and kept on working for her aunt and uncle, she was fine. But her mom? From the looks of the barbed wire, nobody could just walk out of Manzanar.

"We're done here," Akiko said tensely. "Let's go."

"What about your family?" I asked, feeling a pang of homesickness for Vinnie and Baby Lou. "Don't you want to see your brother?"

"Tommy's off fighting in the war," Akiko said. "I don't know where in the world he is right now, but I can guarantee that it's dangerous. People say the Japanese regiment gets sent into the fiercest battles."

I let my eyes wander down the rows of barracks stretching ahead of us. It was hard to understand how Akiko must have been feeling. Her brother was risking his life fighting for freedom over in Europe, while his family, friends, and neighbors were stuck here, in a hot and dusty camp in the desert.

"Akiko, this must be so hard—"

"Lizard!" shrieked Mae. "Wait, no! I mean snake!" And despite being the calmest and coolest of our trio, she leapt into my arms and tried to scale up my shoulders like a cat at bath time. "Get it away from me!"

I jumped too, clinging just as tightly to Mae as she was to my forehead and hair. Then, temporarily losing my mind, I flung myself behind Akiko, hoping she could protect us from the horrible, fork-tongued reptile sunning itself just steps away. But she turned and leapt onto Mae's back, which didn't exactly help my escape.

"A lizard-snake? Is it the Hisser?" I shouted, stumbling backward under the weight of my once-fearless partners. "Do you think he's escaped?"

"Could be!" wailed Mae. "Get away from it!"

"It's just a gopher snake," said Akiko, her usually gravelly voice sounding higher-pitched than I'd ever heard it before. But never one to skip a chance to show off her knowledge, she began to tell us about its habits and history. "It's not venomous the way a rattler is, like the Hisser. But they eat—"

"Enough with the trivia, Akiko! Let's get out of here!"

Without even forming a triangle this time, since we were already tangled like tumbleweed, we transformed in a swirl of purple, green, and orange light. Akiko's sandpaper voice sounded in my ears, and suddenly—thankfully—I felt that familiar stomach drop as we plunged down, down, down. She was teleporting us again, but where?

Five

"WE'RE BACK IN JAPANTOWN?" I ASKED, TURN-
ing in all directions. We were exactly where we'd left,
standing in front of Akiko's old house. "Couldn't you have
returned us to Philadelphia? Or maybe to the beach? Or to
a diner for milkshakes?"

"I was feeling a little pressured," Akiko said, shooting
the stink-eye at Mae. "That Hisser lookalike was a bit too
close for *somebody's* comfort."

"If you are implying that I was the only one uncomfort-
able with a possible supervillain—"

"Button it, you two!" I said, shushing them. "There are

more people on the street now than before, and we don't need to draw more attention to Akiko than necessary."

Suddenly the heavy gray clouds hanging overhead opened up. Fat drops of water hit my arms and head. After the desert heat of Manzanar, Mae and Akiko turned their faces up to it. And I couldn't stop from opening my mouth and catching raindrops on my tongue.

"Let's make a run for that toy shop," Mae called, flinging her hands over her head and trying, but failing, to keep her hair dry.

"No, the place next to it," Akiko said, pulling an umbrella from her bag as the rain began to fall in heavy sheets. "I think it's a diner! I'm hungry!"

"Good idea! Anywhere we can dry off is fine with me," I shouted. Once we caught a break in the traffic, we raced across the street. "It's raining cats and dogs!"

"My mom can't stand thinking of animals stuck in the rain," said Akiko. "She always says, 'It's raining *gnats* and *frogs.*'"

"You and your mom are alike," Mae teased gently, slipping beneath the umbrella with Akiko and me. "Sounds like she avoids dogs too."

We made it inside and scooted into a black vinyl booth, panting and dripping. It was our first chance to rest since this morning in Philadelphia, when we'd grabbed Akiko's hands and teleported across the whole country. I rattled my head at the thought. What would my cousin Kay think about life with superpowers? Though I already knew what her power was: math.

"A couple changes to the menu today, ladies" came the flat drone of a waitress who walked up to our table without even so much as a hello. She'd probably recited this list a hundred times already, judging by her complete lack of enthusiasm. She clicked her gum and never once looked up. In fact, nobody in the booths around us paid Akiko, Mae, or me any attention. Instead, our waitress stared at her notepad, pencil poised and ready to write down our order.

"Sugar rationing just got worse, so our chocolate cake with buttercream frosting is just a chocolate cake—naked, so to speak. No chicken. No lamb. No pork. Though we do have a special on beef tongue sandwiches."

She noisily smacked her gum—*click, click, click*—and waited for our response.

"I . . . ummm . . . ," began Mae, looking a little green.

"Tongue?" Akiko blurted. "You're selling tongue sandwiches—"

I kicked her under the table. My stomach was rumbling, and the last thing I wanted was this waitress to get her nose bent out of joint. The whole country was under tight food rationing. If we insulted her menu, we might have to find our own meal somewhere else. In the rain.

When we couldn't decide, the waitress heaved a sigh

and started to walk away. So I suggested we try starting with something to drink.

"Clam juice, prune juice, tomato juice," she droned. Mae folded her menu with a snap, saying something about heading home to Chicago, where she could get food that tasted good. It was so unlike her typical, well-mannered way that Akiko looked alarmed.

"Wait, I can do this for us," she said, her voice cracking. "Do you have any pie? You know, blueberry? cherry? or maybe apple?"

"No pie." The waitress tapped her pad impatiently. "Pudding."

Once our orders were placed—three banana puddings, nothing to drink—and the waitress disappeared into the kitchen, we settled back into the booth. Mae wanted to get down to business. "Where should we start looking for your mom, Akiko? You don't think she's in trouble, do you?"

Akiko was quiet as she gazed out the window at the rain. Quiet enough, I mean, since I could still hear her fidgeting despite the drumming of the raindrops. "I've been thinking about it," she said with a shrug. "Maybe she's in a nearby town, working on a farm. People have been allowed to leave the camp sometimes, so long as they're doing a service. Like harvesting potatoes or picking cranberries. That's how I got to Philadelphia—to help my aunt and uncle."

If Mam went missing, I could be sure she was doing something for a neighbor or for one of the animals at the vet clinic. Or working an extra shift or a special project with her second job at the shipyard—the way Kay and Jean and the other Secret Six had worked on the top-secret ENIAC project.

"I imagine you're worried about her," said Mae as the waitress set down our puddings. "I haven't seen my daddy in so long. Sometimes I think I might not recognize him walking down the street."

I nodded. It was the same way with me. "Smells bring my dad back," I said. "You know how popcorn smells when you go to the movie theater? When that smell hits my nose, my dad comes flooding back to me. He used to take me to see everything—*The Wizard of Oz* and anything with Katharine Hepburn."

Akiko blew her nose into a hankie, then slipped it back into her bag. "It's funny how certain smells call up a memory," she said, her voice gravelly and low. "Have you ever made cookies with chocolate chips in them? When they're baking, the chips turns all gooey, and your whole house smells like a chocolate cloud. Tommy liked to eat them before they even cooled down."

We sat in silence. Lightning splintered the darkening sky out the window.

"I'll always think of my brother when I smell cookies

in the oven," Akiko said. Then her voice went quieter than usual. "I tried to send him a box. Of cookies, that is. But who knows if he ever got them."

"Where is he fighting?" I asked, picturing my dad in a bomber and flying over the Pacific Ocean.

"Last we heard, he was in Italy," Akiko said. "But news reports say the war is terrible there. So I try not to think too much about it. Which, of course, makes me imagine it in my head all the time—the bombs, the gunfire, the battlefields."

I'd never seen Akiko so serious. That went for Mae, too, who had set down her spoon and was staring into her pudding. My heart clenched at the thought of Mam, my cousin Kay, Vinnie, and Lou.

No matter where Akiko, Mae, and I went—whether it was teleporting across the country or soaring among the clouds—the people we loved came with us. In our minds, in our hearts, and even in the smells we breathed.

"Well, I've got one thing to say about this place," whispered Mae, looking around so our waitress didn't hear. "Popcorn and chocolate-chip cookies sound much better than tongue sandwiches, clam juice, and banana pudding. This stuff stinks like two letters: P-U."

$\mathscr{S}$HE RAIN FINALLY STOPPED, SO WE TOSSED down the right number of coins and left. Akiko pulled a pair of sunglasses from her Hauntima bag and slipped them on. Between them and her umbrella, she was hard to recognize as Japanese. It made walking down the block a little less worrisome.

"Look! They have comic books in this store," said Mae. She was bouncing on her toes as she pointed into the toy shop. "I can see a few of them from here. There's Hauntima and her skull face, Hopscotch on her lime-green scooter. And I can just make it out—there's an issue of the Palomino and Star. Can you see her moonstone ring glowing? And Star's moonstone collar?"

I had the same issue at home. It was probably in the stack of comic books Vinnie and Baby Lou were reading before bedtime, now that I was gone and wouldn't be telling stories to help them fall asleep.

"This place mostly sells dolls," Akiko said, cupping one hand around her sunglasses and peering through the shop's big window. "Dolls from India and from China. England, France, Mexico, Ireland. She's got them big or small, pretty or ugly, baby dolls or fancy dolls."

"How do you know so much about this store?" I asked, trying to avoid another puddle as I moved along the window beside her. "Did you come here a lot before . . . ?" I didn't know how to finish my thought. Before she and her family were sent to the camp? Before the war broke out and changed everything?

"I came for the comic books. But I loved looking at all the toys," Akiko said. She shifted the umbrella from one shoulder to the other. "My mom helped out here when she wasn't working over at my dad's dentist office. Mom is a dressmaker, so she repaired the dolls' gowns, sewed new ones, fixed the hats."

Mae tugged on the door, but it was locked. A note taped above the doorknob read OUT TO LUNCH, BE BACK SOON.

We decided to keep moving along, maybe to another

neighborhood since this one brought back painful memories for Akiko. And since she wasn't supposed to be here anymore. Halfway down the next block, Mae stopped again. This time at a pet store.

"Can we go inside?" she begged. "Please? Look at that bulldog in the window. His eyes! His name is Rocco, and he needs a little love."

Just as she turned the knob to drag us inside, the bulldog leapt off the window bench and growled at us. His jaws snapped, and saliva splattered from his mouth. There was nothing cuddly about him!

"Shut the door!" I called as we jumped backward, our arms and legs tangling up. We nearly tumbled to the ground as we scrambled down the street, racing past benches and bicycles and busy shoppers.

"I'd be happy if I never saw another dog again," panted Akiko once we came to a stop. "Your pal Rocco was scary!"

"Why do you hate dogs so much, Akiko?" asked Mae, catching her breath. "Sure, they make you sneeze. And there are a few scary ones now and then. But how come you can't stand the sight of a dog?"

Akiko's face looked stricken, and she turned away.

"I don't want to talk about it," she mumbled. "Maybe another time."

I could tell Akiko was serious about not wanting to discuss it. She hadn't even given Mae a hard time about naming that pet-store monster. I figured she must have been bitten by a dog when she was little.

We were almost to the corner of the next block now, and I wasn't sure which way to go. The gray clouds hung heavy above us, looking like they could again burst open at any second. We needed to get moving. But just as Mae pointed toward a streetcar, Akiko stopped walking. I accidentally slammed into her.

"What is it?" I asked, trying to hide my annoyance.

"That notice, there on the light pole," she said, her cheeks flushing hot despite the cool San Francisco weather. "It's a secret message!"

Seven

ARENT YOU BEING A LITTLE DRAMATIC?" began Mae as she stepped closer to read the paper nailed to the wooden pole. "It's probably advertising a lost cat."

"Or an art class," I suggested. "Those squiggles could be, well, art!"

Akiko shook her head. "I've never seen anything like this posted around here. And I keep an eye on telephone poles the way Mae's granny looks for overdue books."

We strained to make sense of the writing on the paper, again pressing our heads together beneath Akiko's umbrella so we could see properly. It was just a strip of paper, not a whole page. And the writing wasn't in letters and words. Instead it was what seemed like symbols—it made me think of ancient Egyptian hieroglyphics. As Akiko ran her finger beneath the writing, my eyes tracked along with her, studying each shape.

$$\infty \ \triangle \ |^{\wedge\wedge}| \approx |^{\circ}|$$

"This is almost certainly a coded message," she said, trying to whisper. "But what's it mean?"

"That looks as if the number eight fell on its side," I said quietly. "It reminds me of a toppled snowman."

"And that triangle right there," said Mae, tapping another symbol. "It could be a pyramid."

I stepped back and took a long look around. A street sign indicated we were standing at the corner of Post and Buchanan Streets. I quickly scanned the shops and restaurants in each direction, just to see if a toppled-over snowman or a pyramid were featured on any of the windows, doors, or neon signs. Akiko walked back and forth along the corner doing the same.

"Do you think that number eight could be a symbol for eyeglasses?" asked Mae. "Your dad was a dentist, right, Akiko? Did he have any friends who were eye doctors? Maybe it's a signal for them."

Akiko shook her head. "I don't think so. But that triangle could mean pie!" she said. "What if someone is trying to signal us? To meet them for pie? But we went to the one diner on earth that doesn't serve pie? And now they're sitting there at the right diner, with three slices waiting for us?"

Worry gnawed at my stomach. Which way should we turn? Head east down Post Street and look in every shop for clues to match the message? Or head north on Buchanan Street? Should we split up? Stay together? And what about Akiko being here in Japantown when there were no more Japanese?

"Of course!" shouted Mae suddenly. Her voice caused a few heads to turn in our direction, so she dropped to a whisper. "The number eight on its side—it's not eyeglasses or a fallen snowman. It's a symbol. It stands for infinity!"

Akiko, Mae, and I scrambled back to the telephone pole for another look at the handbill. Our heads knocked into each other as we pushed closer and started reading.

We stared at the looping shape of the infinity symbol. And beside it was that three-sided pyramid. My fingers began to tingle as I touched the paper. Three sides, like a triangle. *Triangle. Tricycle. Triceratops.*

"Tri" meant three of something. As in *trinity.*

"Infinity Trinity," Akiko whispered, tugging the paper from the nails.

She'd been right—this really was a secret message. And even better, it was a secret message meant just for us.

We jumped on the next streetcar, not knowing where we were headed. Akiko folded up her umbrella and slipped it back into her Hauntima bag. Then she flattened the crinkly paper onto her lap, and the three of us studied the symbols penciled onto the page. We turned it upside down, held it up to the light, even licked our fingers and ran them over the writing to test for secret ink.

"Maybe we should hold it to a flame, the way we did for Emmett's note at the diner," suggested Mae. But messing around with matches sounded a little risky, so we dropped that idea.

Eventually the streetcar reached the end of its line. Akiko pointed out the waterfront ahead of us. I saw a long marketplace with a tall tower, which she called the Ferry Building, and a bridge stretching over the blue waves. This bridge was silver instead of orange like the Golden Gate, and Akiko told us it was the Bay Bridge.

Thick suspension cables hung from the towers, forming enormous triangles over the long horizontal stretch of the base. I could see cars driving over San Francisco Bay. The bridge seemed to reach forever into the distance. Beneath it, enormous ships passed in either direction. And on the sidewalk and street around us, traffic was just as busy, with cars, trucks, and people drifting by.

Akiko led us across the street to a bench, where we sat down with the secret message again. A sign indicated we were in Tsunami Sisters Park. I'd never heard of the Tsunami Sisters, but I was glad to see that San Francisco honored its superheroes too. I looked around for a statue, like the one of Zenobia back home in Philadelphia, but all I saw was a fountain with two splashing waterfalls.

Zenobia.

My mind again turned to our last meeting with Mrs. B, when we realized her real identity. When we realized her sister was Zenobia, the greatest superhero the world has ever known. And that it was up to us to find her and bring her back.

"This note," I said, scooting closer to Akiko and Mae on the bench, "almost certainly has to do with superheroes. Think about Mrs. B and what she said last time, at the diner: 'I will be in touch again, most likely quite soon.' This message must be her way of contacting us again! It must be about saving Zenobia!"

Eight

O KAY, LOOK AT THESE SQUIGGLES," BEGAN
Mae, staring at the paper. "Could they be worms? Snakes?"

"Maybe we're supposed to go to the zoo," I suggested. "To
the snake house or something? Or maybe it's hieroglyphics,
and we should go find a museum with mummies—"

"Mommies," whispered Akiko, always interrupting.

"Good idea," said Mae, popping to her feet. "Where's
the nearest museum?"

"No! Over there!" Akiko was on her feet now too, pushing her sunglasses up her nose. "I don't mean mummies. I
really mean *mommies*. As in mine!"

Mae and I scanned the crowd for someone who looked

like a grown-up version of our scrawny, sneezy, asthmatic friend. I saw a clown with a bright red nose, round like an oversize cherry, performing tricks. I noticed two old men seated at a wooden table and playing checkers. Then, over near a flower stand, about a bus length away, I caught sight of her: dark hair, small build, and an expression similar to Akiko's—like she didn't miss a thing.

Ah-choo!

At the sound of Akiko's sneeze, the woman whipped her head in our direction. Mae and I jumped in front of Akiko, blocking her from view like two curtains swinging closed at the theater. Mae pulled us back onto the bench, and I reached into Akiko's Hauntima bag for a comic book to hide behind. The canvas pouch felt ridiculously heavy, which confirmed my suspicion that she really *did* carry around a whole dime store in that thing.

"What are you doing? I need to talk to her," Akiko said, trying to get to her feet again. I settled the bag on the other side of my hip as I held her back. Mae tugged on her arm.

"Slow down, Akiko," she whispered in her gentle kindergarten-teacher voice. "Maybe that lady over there really is your mom. But let's think this through a few steps first."

I flung open the Hopscotch comic book. Together the three of us hid behind it, then peered over the top edge.

"That woman," Akiko said, nodding toward the flower

seller. "I thought I heard someone call her name—Sada. That's my mom's name. I just know that lady is her!"

"How can you be sure?" I whispered. "She could be a stranger who just looks like your mom."

Akiko lowered her sunglasses and squinted, studying the woman.

"Could it really be her?" whispered Mae. "I don't think she sneaked out of the internment camp and caught a train back to San Francisco. Do you?"

"No way," Akiko said. "You saw it—those camps have barbed wire and watchtowers and guns. Nobody does anything like that. It's too dangerous."

We sat in silence for a few moments. Well, close to silence. Akiko's breathing was fast. And then Mae caught sight of two puppies wrestling on the grass not far from us. I could tell she was trying hard not to pay attention to them, but I heard her let out a faint "*awwww*."

"So if that's really your mom," I began. "And if she's supposed to be in a camp somewhere far away from here . . ." I paused. "And if she didn't tell anyone at the camp about leaving, which is why someone wrote that letter your cousin showed us, then . . . ?"

Mae and I looked warily at each other over Akiko's head.

"Then what in the world is your mom doing?" asked Mae, staring wide-eyed at the woman near the flower stand.

Akiko tried to jump to her feet again. "I've got to ask her!"

Mae and I grabbed her shoulders and pulled her back down.

"Akiko, you can't. Not without getting all three of us into trouble," Mae said, keeping her voice steady but trying to get through our friend's thick, stubborn, know-it-all head. "We've got to wait and see what she's doing. My granny might not be too understanding if she gets a phone call that I'm all the way in California!"

"Don't be a knucklehead, Akiko," I whispered, though maybe I was as loud as Akiko. "You're supposed to be in Philadelphia. What's your mom going to think about you waltzing around San Francisco?"

"She'd think," Akiko said, finally falling back against the bench in surrender, "that I was probably up to something."

"And she'd be right," whispered Mae, adjusting the comic book to better shield us from view. "Because now that we've got that secret message, we really *are* up to something. Plus, our minds should be on Zenobia. She needs us to save her!"

I was about to add something about Mrs. B needing us to save her, too, but the sound of bagpipes caught my attention. I sat up again, looking around. Suddenly more bagpipes joined in, and the shrill wheezing of a marching band let us know that a parade had arrived.

"Do you hear that, Akiko?" teased Mae. "Bagpipes sound a little like you do when you really get going."

Akiko laughed before ribbing back at Mae. "See that boy plugging his ears to keep the noise out? That's a little like me too, when you start talking about animals and what they're thinking."

I laughed, happy to be in the middle of their back-and-forth this time. Maybe we were growing more comfortable with each other, because Mae and Akiko seemed to be a lot funnier than they were in Philadelphia.

"And look at that one there, marching with the big baton and blowing the whistle," one of them said.

"The leader?" said the other. "That's a lot like Josie, bossing—"

"No," I said sharply, clutching Akiko's arm.

"What, Josie? Can't you take a little teasing?"

"Teasing is fine," I said quickly, looking in all directions. "It's your mom, Akiko. She's gone!"

Nine

ONCE THE PARADE PASSED, I FOCUSED ON the flower seller again. But the woman Akiko believed was her mother was nowhere to be seen.

"Josie's right," said Akiko, who had climbed onto a bench for a better view. "We've lost her!"

"Did you catch a glimpse of who she was with?" I asked, climbing up beside Akiko and craning my neck to see up and down the street. "Maybe her friends are somewhere around here."

Mae tugged the two of us back down. "I know you want to help, Josie, however you can. You're bighearted that way." Then, looking intently at Akiko, she squeezed her hand. "And

I know you want to find out what's happening with your mom, Akiko. But we're the Infinity Trinity now. Somebody is trying to reach us with this coded message! They could be in danger!"

Akiko rattled her head as if clearing her mind, then reached into her Hauntima bag. "Maybe that wasn't even my mom," she said, pulling out the crinkled message and handing it to Mae. "Maybe I'm letting my imagination get the better of me."

"Don't worry, Akiko. We'll still keep a lookout for anyone who resembles your mom," I assured her. "Family's important." I didn't have to remind them that family was the reason for everything we did.

The horn from a passing ship let out a deep bellow, signaling to the other boats nearby. It drew our attention to the bay, and the three of us began walking on a pathway that skirted the water's edge. We were silent as we gazed out at the ships. A seagull bobbed on the lapping water, and each wave brought in a slight smell of the sea.

"That's a battleship," observed Mae. "Other than the ship we saved from the Hisser, I've never seen one so close. I wonder why it's coming into the bay."

"It's enormous," marveled Akiko, kicking off her black-and-white saddle shoes and socks. She reached into her Hauntima bag, pulled out a pair of summer sandals, and slid her feet into them. Then she started noisily banging the soles of her saddle shoes together like cymbals, getting rid of the dust and grime from the Manzanar camp.

As I watched her tuck the saddle shoes back into her canvas pouch, I considered asking if she had two more pairs of sandals in there for Mae and me. Or even better, two extra pairs of sunglasses. But I didn't think her bag could possibly hold so much stuff.

"Look farther down into the bay," I said, squinting as I pointed south along the waterfront. "There are even more ships down there. I think they're fixing a submarine over at that one. See it?"

We gazed up and down the coast. Everywhere I looked, I saw another dock and another enormous boat painted gray. A whisper of worry raced down my spine at the thought of a villain like the Hisser trying to destroy them. Ships like these were important in the war effort, both here in the Pacific Ocean and overseas in England and France.

"That one right there is a cruiser," explained Mae. She was like Vinnie when she did this, exhaling little facts like she was breathing. "Cruisers are the second biggest military ships after aircraft carriers. And that one is—"

"It's a destroyer," interrupted Akiko. She was never going to let Mae out-fact her. If Vinnie suddenly arrived, I wondered which one of them would drive me cuckoo first. "Destroyers escort other ships and convoys, carry torpedoes, hunt submarines."

As we walked farther along the shoreline, I gazed out at the water and the ships gracefully gliding by. While the sight of the enormous battleships was impressive, I still preferred smaller boats. Like sailboats and even rowboats. They reminded me of playing in the park when I was younger. My dad and I used to fold up sheets of paper into tiny rafts. We could spend hours setting those sturdy little boats onto the pond, right on the edge of the lapping water.

Lapping water.

I froze, midstep. Then I grabbed Akiko and Mae each by the arm. I couldn't take my eyes off the water's edge ahead of us and the waves at the shore. They rolled in, one after the next. Wave upon wave.

"Josie, what is it?" asked Mae.

"Are you getting sick?" croaked Akiko. "Was it that banana pudding?"

It took me a minute to find my voice. "Quick, open up the note. I think we've got something!"

Mae flattened out the handbill. After hanging on the pole in Japantown, the paper wanted to curl up like a roly-poly. Again we stared at the cryptic symbols.

$$\infty \; \Delta \; |^{\wedge\wedge}| \approx |^{\circ}|$$

"What did you figure out?" asked Akiko, her voice sand-paper.

"Waves," I said, nearly shouting. "What if those two squiggly lines represent waves? Like these!"

I flung my arms wide, taking in the scope of the whole San Francisco Bay and the ships on the water.

"That's good, Josie. You could be right!" said Mae. She held the note out at arm's length and studied the symbols even more intently. "The squiggles really do look like waves. And this . . . ?"

Suddenly she gasped, raising the paper a few inches and lowering it again—up, down, up, down. She did this a few more times as Akiko and I watched in confusion.

"What?" said Akiko. "Mae, what are you doing?"

"Two towers, suspension wires, and a base!" she shouted, still holding the message out in front of her. "The bridge! It's one of the clues!"

We stared again. Akiko read aloud as I ran my finger beneath each symbol.

$$\infty \ \triangle \ |^{\wedge\wedge}| \approx |^{\circ}|$$

"Infinity. Trinity. Bay Bridge. Lapping water," she said. Then she tapped the paper at the last symbol. "But what's this? A circle inside an upright rectangle? Is it a ship?"

Mae spun around so her back was to the water now. She held the secret message out and moved slowly along the skyline of the city, as if testing to see whether it would catch in the sunlight.

"Maybe it's a coffee cup?" I said, trying to think creatively. "A tomato sandwich? A fried egg? What do you think about—"

Wheeze!

Akiko interrupted with a raspy intake of air. I wasn't sure exactly what sound she was making—it was a little like a bagpipe. Not her usual sneeze or cough or rapid-fire talking. Mae thumped her on the back, looking alarmed.

Akiko raised her sunglasses up into her hair, then pointed just above the top edge of the paper. Unable to speak, she just gestured and gasped. So Mae and I followed her finger to some spot in the distance where she was pointing.

"What, Akiko?" I asked. "Tell us!"

"There," she sputtered. "That's it!"

It took a moment for my eyes to adjust. She was pointing toward a tall tower standing not far from us. I'd heard her call it the Ferry Building. My eyes darted back to the paper, then up again—back and forth.

$$\infty \; \triangle \; |^{\wedge\wedge}| \; \approx \; |^{\circ}|$$

"Rectangle," whispered Mae. "That tower is a rectangle."

And smack in the center of it sat a big, round clock.

"And a circle," I said, my finger on the secret message. I tried not to shout for joy. "Brilliant, Akiko!"

"Not just me. We found it together," she croaked. "This note is telling us to go to the Ferry Building! Beside the water and the bridge! I bet it's from Mrs. B!"

The clock's bells began to chime, marking the top of the hour. *Gong! Gong!*

"It's only two o'clock," I said, looping my arms through theirs and setting off for the tall tower rising from the Ferry Building. "I have a feeling something really big is going to happen here in San Francisco."

W E'D GONE ONLY A SHORT DISTANCE WHEN a shadow fell on the ground in front of us. A really big shadow. It was round and long and slow-moving, like a blimp or a zeppelin. The three of us froze.

"What is that?" whispered Mae, motionless as a rabbit.

"I don't think it's a solar eclipse," answered Akiko.

I looked up. The sun's glare was dizzying, despite the gray clouds.

"I don't see anything," I said, turning like a beam in a lighthouse, my head tilted back.

Ka-boom!

The crowd along the waterfront began to scream and

run in all directions. Akiko, Mae, and I looked hard into one another's faces. Innocent people could get hurt. Without speaking a word, we each knew what the other two were thinking: We had to do something.

"There it is," I yelled, pointing into the sky just west of us. "But I have no idea *what* it is!"

"It looks like a balloon," said Mae, her voice sounding puzzled. "But I've never seen one so enormous."

"And it's got all those smaller balloons hanging off it," observed Akiko.

We watched as one of the smaller balloons dropped from the bigger one. Moments later, we heard another explosion.

Ka-BOOM!

"It's a b-bomb-dropping balloon!" I stammered, barely comprehending the words as I spoke them. "We've got to do something to stop it!"

Tee-hee-heee!

The sound of laughter hit me like a bucket of ice water. I couldn't stop the quick shiver of fear that raced down my back. That laugh reminded me of the Hisser back in Philadelphia.

Not far from us, a street performer I'd seen earlier was pointing at the sky and laughing. He was dressed like a clown in a round bowler hat, with wild hair sticking out from beneath it in springy curls. His nose was a cherry-red bulb, and his face was painted to exaggerate his eyes and mouth. His bright red lips circled upward, in a forced smile.

A single word popped into my head: *dangerous.*

"I hate clowns," I whispered. "What does anybody find funny about them?"

"Their shoes are funny," offered Mae quickly, always looking for the positive. "And they sometimes have funny gags, like slipping on a banana peel or squirting water out of a flower."

The clown had been shaking hands with a white-haired grandfather. But the grandpa was jerking his hand away, as if shocked by electricity. This clown must have been using one of those buzzer rings, the kind that sends a quick jolt into another person's hand. As the clown kept on with his noisy laugh, the grandpa cringed and stumbled away. He didn't look amused at all.

"What's so funny about that?" said Akiko. "Clowns are obnoxious."

I looked back into the sky at the balloon as another explosion boomed. So far, the deadly smaller balloons had only hit the water. But what if they fell onto something else? "That thing could wind up bombing one of the warships! Or one of the bridges!"

"Or one of us!" echoed Mae.

Again the clown nearby let out a sinister laugh as people of all ages raced past him, looking for cover. He hopped up onto a picnic table and kept his eyes on the balloon bomb, as if guiding it in some way.

"Get ready for fireworks, people!" His shoulders shook as he laughed. "This should be a real show!"

Suddenly, all around us, other clowns swarmed the waterfront. They wore the same bowler hat, oversize shoes, and red nose as the first clown.

"We are at your command, Side-Splitter."

Side-Splitter?

"Did you hear those other clowns?" I whispered, nudging Mae and Akiko. "They're ready to do his bidding?"

"Wait a minute," hissed Akiko in a loud whisper. "Those new clowns look a whole lot like that one standing on the picnic table! They seem to be other versions of him."

Akiko was right. The clowns flooding the pavement around us were just like the first one, only some were a little taller, some shorter, many were heavier. But they all had the same basic appearance as the dangerous-looking one called Side-Splitter.

"Replication," Mae whispered. "He's no ordinary clown! He's got superpowers to split off new versions of himself over and over again. To form—"

"A clown army!" choked Akiko.

Ka-BOOM!

Another explosion echoed across the water, this time closer to the Bay Bridge. We had to act, and fast.

Without a word, we ducked away from the crowd, racing past a few parked cars to the other side of a delivery truck. Nobody was around, so we stepped in close together to form our familiar triangle.

"This villain is going to require everything we've got," whispered Mae as we grabbed hands. "It's up to us to fight him, whether Hauntima's ghost helps us or not!"

We transformed again, in the whirl of golden light that mixed with swirling streams of orange, purple, and green. When we dropped back to the ground and caught our footing, I patted my boots and ran my fingers across my mask, checking my equipment to make sure it was battle-ready.

"Let's take out that balloon bomb first," Akiko said, her eyes on the round menace drifting through the sky, "before it destroys the bridge."

"Then it's on to Side-Splitter," I said, pushing away any doubts or fears. "We've got to stop his clown army."

Just as we were about to jump into action, something on the ground beside us caught my eye. It must have fallen from Akiko's bag. It was her comic book, and the final whoosh of wind from our transformation sent the pages fluttering. It opened to the image of a green-and-yellow-caped figure riding a bright lime-green scooter.

Mae and Akiko saw it too, and as I bent to pick it up, the three of us whispered her name at precisely the same moment:

"Hopscotch."

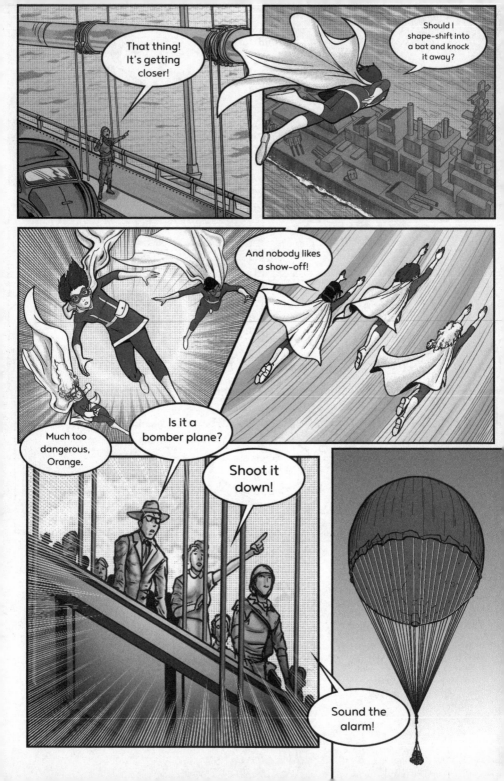

Twelve

AKIKO, MAE, AND I SWOOPED OVER THE waterfront and around the Ferry Building, sizing up the scene for what was ahead. Were we really going to battle a deranged clown and his red-nosed army? I tried to swallow, but my mouth was too dry. Instead, all the moisture seemed to have gone to my hands, which were sweating inside my green gloves.

Mae pointed down at Side-Splitter. He was tossing three or four bright-colored juggling balls into the air like he was entertaining crowds at a circus. Not far from him, a few of his clown copies stretched a wide rubber band across two light poles. I had no idea what they were up to, but I was certain it would be trouble.

Whoosh!

"Duck!" shouted Akiko as one of the juggling balls whipped through the air like cannon fire. Two more followed in quick succession. "It's a slingshot!"

We watched the balls hit the side of the silver bridge and explode.

"We can't let him destroy San Francisco!" I shouted.

"How can we stop those deadly cannonballs?" hollered Akiko, swooping back toward Side-Splitter. "I'll try setting them ablaze before they reach their target!"

But suddenly more slingshots were firing at us and more juggling balls were hurtling through the air. Akiko flew like a hummingbird, darting this way and that as she flung fire at the swarm of deadly cannonballs.

"I can slow down those clown copies," hollered Mae, wiggling her fingers as if she were sitting down to play a piano concert. "I'll pummel them with hail—the big kind, too, the size of grapefruit."

And as she thrust both her hands forward, low clouds swept in from the east. Seconds later, I heard a heavy patter start up. It sounded like marbles spilling across a floor, only much louder. Icy chunks of rain, the same size and shape as grapefruits, dropped from the sky and beaned the clowns on their bowler hats, backs, and arms, and sent them running for shelter.

Side-Splitter waved an angry fist into the air.

"Curses on you, Infinite Irritants!" he wailed.

Now it was my turn. I quickly considered the best strategy for attack. Use my superstrength to carry off Side-Splitter and throw him in the water? Maybe use my flying powers to zoom in fast and low over their heads, knocking off their bowler hats?

"I've got it!" I whispered.

Watching Akiko fling fire at the clowns' explosive cannonballs, I could see that half were getting past her and pounding into the support towers of the Bay Bridge. So I fixed my eyes on the nearest red ball and followed its arc through the sky. Concentrating as hard as I could, I flicked my eyes to the right.

"Did you see that?" shouted Akiko as she soared past me. "That cannonball just curved back on itself, like a boomerang!"

I wanted to tell her that I did see it. But if I let myself get distracted, I'd lose track of the dangerous cannonball. So instead I concentrated all my mental powers, forcing it to crash into the ground beside Side-Splitter.

Blam!

It exploded on the cement plaza. Side-Splitter and his clowns dodged the flames and the hail of ice hammering down from Mae. In a desperate frenzy, they tried to launch more cannonballs. But our efforts seemed to be slowing them down.

"How about a little company up there, kiddies?" shrieked Side-Splitter.

Immediately, something moving in the air to my left, enormous and round, caught my attention. It was another balloon bomb! He seemed to be pulling the deadly orb closer to us. It dropped one, two, three bombs from its ropes. After just a few moments, three explosions burst on the water below.

Boom! Boom! Boom!

One of us would have to stop this thing, but who?

"Hauntima's ghost," Akiko shouted. "This guy is trying to destroy us!"

"Hauntima's ghost is exactly what we need!" I hollered back, feeling the heat from the explosion. Then, cupping my hands to my mouth, I called, "If you're out there, Hauntima, we could use a little help!"

Akiko spun through the air like a gymnast and launched fire from both her hands to stop another battering of Side-Splitter's cannonballs. "What if Hauntima's too weak?" she croaked.

Mae scooped the air around her in a circular motion, as if stirring something to life. The hailstorm took on a new intensity. "I wish somebody could help us!" she said. "I don't know how much longer we can hang on!"

Suddenly, I caught the distinct sound of another noise. Blending in with the booming explosions, the rising shouts, and the maniacal laughter, it was faint at first. But then it grew clearer, riding to my ears on the whipping wind.

It was the whir of a motor.

Beep, beep!

I took my eyes off another cannonball for just a second to peer toward the Ferry Building. And my heart hiccupped in my chest at what I saw: a lime-green scooter speeding along the pathway.

"I can't believe it!" shouted Mae, who must have seen it too.

"Is that really her?" followed Akiko.

Hopscotch!

Moments later, green and yellow flashed toward us as the star of Akiko's comic book arrived. She conjured squares out of thin air and flung them ahead of her. Her tall yellow boots landed on each one just a split second after it appeared, as Hopscotch climbed her magic staircase through the sky.

"Hey, I didn't think Hopscotch had superpowers," said Mae in a noisy whisper. "In her comic books, it seems like she only does karate—"

"I told you she had powers," answered Akiko. "She's a master at karate *and* she can conjure whatever she needs—"

"Save it for later, you two!" I said, interrupting their

debate. "We have a few more important things to handle!"

Hopscotch reached us in a matter of seconds. Her hands planted on her hips, she surveyed the chaos below. "This clown is a real riot," she said. "And I mean that in the worst possible way."

Thirteen

HOPSCOTCH'S BOXY YELLOW MASK SHROUDED her eyes, but I could tell she was angry. Her coloring was as faint as Hauntima's had been, so I knew she was merely a ghostly version of herself too.

"How long has this deranged knee-slapper been at it?" she asked, cracking her knuckles beneath lime-green gloves. "Think he's tiring out?"

We shook our heads. No way. Side-Splitter seemed to be just getting started. And judging by his attacks, he wanted to wreck the whole waterfront.

"He's pounding the Bay Bridge," Akiko explained. "And we can figure he's set on hitting the Golden Gate Bridge, too."

"With his own clown army to wage his battles," added Mae. "Side-Splitter's going to be tough to beat!"

"Hopscotch," I said, "do you think we're strong enough to stop him?"

She gazed at the three of us for a beat or two. "Strong enough? Strength doesn't mean physical power. Strength means never giving up, no matter how hard the fight. And from what I know of the Infinity Trinity, you're not the kind to surrender."

She flung more squares ahead of her and raced higher over the scene. Akiko, Mae, and I flew quickly behind. Another explosion thundered, and the shouting grew even louder.

"The best way to handle a clown like this is with a dose of his own medicine," Hopscotch said. Her fragile voice barely reached our ears amid the chaos. We hovered closer, hanging on her words. "But my abilities are limited. It's up to you, Infinity Trinity."

Without warning, a jolt of electricity shot through the air. Akiko and Mae dodged right and left out of its path. And at the last moment, I ducked too. But a smell like burnt toast stung my nose. I looked down below to see Side-Splitter pointing his buzzer ring right at the three of us.

"He can pull those balloon bombs through the sky *and* shoot electricity?" shouted Mae.

"Electromagnetism," answered Akiko. There was no

time for showing off, but I knew she was proud to demon-
strate her knowledge of superpowers. "Looks like he's got
one of the most powerful abilities out there—attracting and
repelling metal and controlling electricity, too."

Side-Splitter stared up at us, enraged.

But then he seemed to recognize Hopscotch's green-
and-yellow form. "What's this? It looks like the ghostly
figure of my old friend from the playground." Then, his
voice low and menacing, Side-Splitter warned, "Hopscotch,
your turn is over."

Suddenly, he fired two more electrical jolts through the
air toward Hopscotch. Without ducking, she spun around
and stared at Side-Splitter. And as if from thin air, she
conjured a dainty fan and whipped it open. Fanning herself
like some Southern lady, she deflected his shot.

"You're still the same," she called, though her voice was
weak. "A little off."

And with that, the fight was on again.

Akiko let loose a burst of flames that caught three of the
clowns' juggling balls just as they launched. They exploded
over Side-Splitter and his copies, raining down ash and
embers onto their heads.

"Good one, Orange Inferno!" cheered Hopscotch, her
ghostly fists punching the air.

And she jumped into action too, her hands moving as if
she were dealing cards. With quick flicks of her wrist, she

flung cream pies into stack after stack, conjuring them up right before my eyes.

"Emerald Shield," Hopscotch shouted, "hop to it!"

At first I hadn't a clue what I was supposed to do. So I picked up a pie and turned it around in my hands. But knowing I had superstrength, I decided to hurl it at Side-Splitter with all the force I could muster. The pie hit with a squelchy smack that was surprisingly satisfying! I picked up as many as I could and began pitching them at the clowns, one after another, like I was a baseball player.

Side-Splitter fumed.

"Pie for breakfast . . ." He snarled as another cream pie hit him in the face.

"Pie for lunch," he went on ominously. When he paused, I hit him with a banana cream that had the tallest whipped topping I'd ever seen. Part of me wanted to call a time-out so Mae, Akiko, Hopscotch, and I could taste one.

"And pie," he said bitterly, his words slow and menacing, "for dinner."

Without warning, Side-Splitter flicked his fingers at Hopscotch and me. We leapt aside just in time. But behind us, I heard an explosion over the water. His electromagnetic jolts rained down flames and smoke onto the choppy waves.

"Don't lose heart, Infinity Trinity," Hopscotch called to us. "It's only when we're tested that we can see what we're really made of!"

Mae circled tightly in the air. Seagulls seemed to be gliding closer to her. I slowed my pie throwing and sneaked a quick glance. It looked as if Mae was speaking to the birds. What was she doing?

"Are you kidding?" hollered Akiko, sounding frantic as she dodged more of Side-Splitter's electrical jolts. "This is no time for chatting with animals!"

But Mae appeared to have given the gulls orders, because they began to dive toward Side-Splitter like a squadron of bomber planes. They pecked at his red nose, attacking his hat and his hair in a chaotic frenzy.

"Get away from me," he wailed, swatting blindly at his head.

Mae must have summoned more birds because, without warning, pelicans appeared, followed by hawks, herons, and even hummingbirds. Flock after flock, they swooped down on Side-Splitter again and again, sending him shrieking with rage.

"Well done, Violet Vortex," cheered Hopscotch, though her voice didn't carry far. "You have a gift for organization."

"And you seem to have another superpower," Akiko added, though I couldn't tell if she was excited or keeping score on who had more.

"Looks like all your chatting with dogs was part of something bigger," I called, grateful to see Side-Splitter thrown off-balance. "Thanks for the distraction!"

Just as I swooped around to the other side of Hopscotch, a cry went up. But it wasn't Side-Splitter this time. It was a bird. Its wing appeared to be broken, probably from the fight with our crazed clown.

As it dropped through the sky, helpless and unable to fly, I reached out and caught it.

"Shhh," I whispered, gently cupping my hands around its small body. "You're going to be all right." I could feel its heart thumping like a motor against my fingers. It seemed to be a woodpecker, judging by its sharp beak and bright red crown.

I pressed the terrified bird to my cheek to calm it. And then, closing my eyes and focusing my mind, I concentrated as hard as I could. I imagined the black-and-white-striped feathers of its injured wing and pictured it flapping again.

When I opened my eyes and uncupped my hands, the bird took flight.

"Did you just—" shouted Akiko, her voice sounding surprised.

"Emerald Shield, watch out!"

But Mae's warning was replaced by a dizzying blast in my ears. Suddenly, my body seemed to be in a free fall, spiraling downward through the sky.

Hopscotch's voice was the last thing I heard. "She's been hit!"

Fourteen

"HER LEG IS STICKING OUT AT A WEIRD angle."

"Give her room, please!"

"It's one of those superhero kids. From that Endless Trio or whatever they're called."

The voices came to me slowly, as if from far away. I tried to open my eyes, but the glare was too strong.

"Emerald Shield, can you hear me?"

That last voice sounded gravelly, like she had sandpaper in her throat.

Akiko!

Opening my eyes, I gazed up at an orange mask. It

was covering familiar eyes that looked pained with worry. I tried to sit up, but the world seemed to be spinning like a merry-go-round. I wanted off.

"Take it slowly," came another voice. This one was Mae's. She was crouching over me now, beside Akiko. I could read the worry on her face too.

"Your leg appears to be broken." Hopscotch gave my arm a squeeze, and I felt a wave of gratitude that she was here too. "You must be hurting."

"Let me see," I said with a grimace as Mae and Akiko helped pull me up to a sitting position. My legs stretched out on the cement ground before me. My green boots looked shiny, but one was pointing off in a direction that seemed wrong. I ran my hands along my broken leg, wrapping my fingers around the area that hurt the most. But before I could speak up, a laugh sliced the air.

Tee-hee-heee!

"Side-Splitter," Akiko shouted, jumping to her feet. "He's getting away!"

"One down, two more to go!" came his menacing call. "Plus my old pal Hopscotch!"

I heard the squeal of tires and the slamming of a door. Then a truck barreled off. "Don't worry," came his unsettling shout, "I'll be back. The fun's only just begun!"

The crowd let out a groan, and I noticed it was just everyday people and tourists now. Gone were the funny hats and big red noses of Side-Splitter's replicated clowns.

"Don't move, Emerald Shield," hollered Akiko. "I can shape-shift into a stretcher! Or crutches! Or a cane!"

"Or I could ask a horse to carry you," offered Mae, gently patting my shoulder.

I rubbed my hands over my shin and knee, and closed my eyes again. Concentrating all my energy, I focused on making the knife-hot pain in my leg disappear.

"I'm feeling a little better," I said, reaching for Akiko's and Mae's hands. "Can you help me up?"

They got me to my feet again, letting me wrap an arm over each of their shoulders for support. As much as the fight with Side-Splitter had rattled me, I was grateful to have Mae and Akiko at my side. Whatever was to come, we'd do it together.

I took a few steps, and suddenly the crowd began to clap and cheer. I could hardly believe what was happening.

"It's not so bad now," I said, looking from my orange partner to my purple one. "In fact, I think it's healed!"

"Really?" Akiko said, kneeling for a closer look at my leg. "I can't believe it. I saw it myself—your leg was broken!"

Mae cautioned me not to push myself too hard. But my leg was already back to normal. I thought about the woodpecker I'd caught during the battle. Its wing seemed broken when I'd first held it.

"I admire your perseverance—all three of you," Hopscotch

said, gazing first at Mae, then Akiko, then me. "Don't let setbacks discourage you. It's when we're challenged that we learn how high we can soar."

I took Hopscotch's hand in mine and thanked her. Mae and Akiko did too. Even though Side-Splitter got away, we'd given him a good fight. I was grateful for Hopscotch's help.

Mae spoke something to a few of the birds who were lingering overhead. She must have let them know I was better, since they took off in a whirl, sending a puff of feathers into the air.

"Can you believe her? Talking to animals?" Akiko said, shaking her head. "And you have another power too, Emerald Shield. Healing is going to come in very handy."

Hopscotch jumped onto her scooter and revved the engine. Throwing a wave goodbye over her shoulder, she zoomed off through the crowd. "Side-Splitter will be back soon. And so will I!"

WE WATCHED HOPSCOTCH GO. THEN CON-
fusion seemed to break out all around us. People began
to shout and carry on as the damage from Side-Splitter's
reckless attack started to register.

Smoke hung around the Bay Bridge, and emergency
crews raced to put out flames on the boats he'd set on fire
in the water. The frantic crowd pushed in closer to us, and
it became clear we needed to get away. We nodded to each
other and slipped off from the crowd. In seconds, we were
back in the air again.

"Look," shouted someone near us. "It's those kid superheroes."

"There they go," cheered another one, pointing at our shapes as we crossed the sky over the waterfront. "I've read about them! They're called the Infinity Trinity!"

"Finally!" yelled Akiko. And she turned a few corkscrew spins in excitement. "Hauntima's ghost! It's about time somebody got our name right!"

A wet wind off the bay whipped our capes as the three of us circled the city. Before that run-in with Side-Splitter and the balloon bombs, we'd been solving the clues written on that secret message from Japantown. Akiko, Mae, and I had been heading toward the Ferry Building and, I'd hoped, to Mrs. B. Now I was more eager than ever for a chance to talk with her again.

"Mrs. B is probably wondering what's taking us so long," called Mae. "Let's hurry up and get inside that building."

We soared over the city's hills and parks, keeping an eye out for Side-Splitter and any of his duplicate clowns, until we reached the Golden Gate Bridge. Then we dropped low and skirted the shoreline all the way back to the ferry boats. After a few minutes, Akiko pointed to what seemed like the perfect place to land.

"On the far side of the Ferry Building's roof," she called. "There must be a door to that clock tower."

After a shaky landing—we needed to make adjustments for the unpredictable gusts of wind and a surprising number of seagulls—we were back in our everyday clothes. Mae and I followed Akiko across the rooftop toward the tall, rectangular tower and the circular clockface. They looked just like the shapes penciled onto the message.

I smiled as I imagined Mrs. B drawing each symbol.

"It's locked," Akiko announced, bringing our rush to a complete halt. She rattled the door a few more times just to make sure. But it didn't budge. "Maybe we should have teleported inside the building."

"No way," argued Mae. "We can't just go around popping out of thin air into strangers' offices."

"It would have been better than this," Akiko said. "Getting stuck on a rooftop."

As usual, I was caught in the middle of their back-and-forth. I stared at the doorknob and tried to think. There had to be a way around this—or actually through it, since it was a heavy locked door.

"Can either of you pick a lock?" I asked, giving the door another try.

That caught their attention. Puzzle solving was a real passion for all three of us. And not all puzzles were on paper. I was pretty confident that, like me, Akiko and Mae had some extra skills to share.

Mae slipped a hairpin from one of her curls. "I've been doing this for years," she whispered. "Step aside." And she began to tinker with the knob, twisting the hairpin and listening for a *click*.

"This is awfully sneaky," observed Akiko as she peered over Mae's shoulder. I could tell she was impressed. "Does your granny know you can pick locks?"

"Who do you think taught me?" Mae replied. "Granny Crumpler is a librarian of many talents."

It took Mae only a few flicks and twists to get past the lock. Then we were inside the Ferry Building and racing down the iron staircase. As we reached the floor below, I heard the clacking of typewriting machines. It reminded me a little of the sounds in the Moore School's hallway, when we found Kay and the other human computers working on the calculators. One long hallway stretched to our left, another to our right. Lettering was painted on the frosted glass at each door, indicating what type of business was inside.

I pointed at the first door to our left. The window glass read T. D. LYNCH, ATTORNEY AT LAW. "Think this is some sort of code for Room Twelve?" I whispered.

Mae and Akiko shook their heads as we crept past the next few doors. We passed words and names that seemed innocent enough: DUNCAN & DAVIS DISTRIBUTORS, something about an import-export business, and then another about an accounting firm.

"This one," Akiko said, running her finger under PARIDA & FLEMING, TAILORS. "Do you think those letters scramble up into 'Room Twelve Enterprises'? Or something like that?"

We didn't have time to unscramble possible clues, because suddenly a door we'd just passed was opening. Two cigar-smoking men stepped out into the hall with us. They were deep in conversation, so we took the opportunity to hurry ahead of them. But their gruff voices and cigar smoke seemed to trail close behind.

"You kids," one of them finally called. "What are you moppets doing here? Are you lost?"

Though they seemed friendly enough, I didn't want to stick around to find out. I shot farther ahead, forcing myself not to run, but to move along the hallway in the fastest walk I could muster. Mae and Akiko were on either side of me doing the same.

"Pick one," I whispered as we passed more doors. "We've got to scram, right now!"

"You do it," Akiko whispered back. "What if we get in trouble for barging in?"

"We're about to get in trouble for being in this hallway," added Mae through her teeth. Her usually calm voice sounded high and tight. "So one of us has to open one of these doors. Immediately!"

As the next doorknob came into sight on my left, I grabbed it and whipped it open. Akiko and Mae were so close on my heels, we tumbled inside and onto the floor like dominoes. I heard the men's laughter disappear down the hall, their footsteps echoing on the staircase.

When we straightened up, the noisy *tap-tap-ding* sound of the typewriters at the desks all around us came to an abrupt halt. The office went silent as a church—or maybe Granny Crumpler's library.

"May we help you?" asked the lady closest to us. Her fingers hovered just above her typewriter keys, as if she wanted to keep this quick and get back to work.

So did I.

"We're looking for her uncle," Akiko began confidently. She hooked a thumb at me. "Uncle Les. He works around here. Runs a talent company?"

What was Akiko thinking? I jabbed her with my elbow.

She jabbed right back.

The finger-hovering typist started to give us the brush-off, but another one pushed back from her cluttered desk and came around to greet us.

"Uncle Les, huh?" She laughed. "You must mean Leslie Christmas. He's the biggest name in local theater—everybody knows him. And his cigar! His office is just down the hall."

I raised my eyebrows at Akiko, who stuck her nose in the air now, as if she'd known what she was doing all along. Mae was just as astounded. Without uttering a word, she mouthed questions to Akiko. *How? Who? Why?*

"Didn't you hear those two cigar smokers who were behind us?" whispered Akiko—or at least she tried to whisper—as the typist led the three of us back into the hallway. "One of them was named Les."

Mae tried to hide her smile, but I could hear it in her voice. "You were eavesdropping," she whispered. "Who's the sneaky one now?"

I shushed them both, since this was no time to compare snooping skills. The question was whether any of this would help us find Room Twelve. The friendly typist was walking briskly up ahead. But then another door opened, and a figure stepped into the hallway. I hardly glanced in that direction. Until I heard her speak.

The familiar voice stopped us in our tracks.

"Come along, Astra. It's time for your walk."

Sixteen

$\mathcal{G}$IRLS! WHAT IN THE WORLD ARE YOU DOING here?"

Mrs. B was fuming as she shut the door to the hallway. Once she and Astra had gotten over their shock at stumbling into our trio, they ushered us into what must have been Room Twelve's offices.

Looking around the busy space, I was reminded of what we'd seen in Philadelphia. The heavy curtains were drawn tight, maps hung on every wall, desks were pushed together in the back, men and women wearing headsets crisscrossed the room, and radios transmitted news reports in a variety of languages.

"How did you find us?" snapped Mrs. B, handing off Astra's leash to an assistant. "We purposely *did not* send for the Infinity Trinity."

We fell silent. This was not the warm reception I was expecting.

"Wh-what do you mean, Mrs. B?" My voice was a little unsteady. I cleared my throat and tried to speak up. "We found your note."

"It was a good one," Mae added with one of her sunny smiles. But Mrs. B would have none of it. She scowled at us like we were trick-or-treaters in July.

"Note? What note?" she asked tightly. "I did not leave you a note."

"In Japantown. Nailed to a telephone pole," croaked Akiko. "You must remember. The clues were so clever. Especially the one about this tower."

Astra let out a bark and jumped up to perch beside us. I noticed he was sitting on the steamer trunk I'd carried from the fire in Philadelphia. Astra seemed to be moving a little more stiffly than he had before, and I wondered if he was tired. I reached over and scratched his ears.

"Well, if you didn't leave the message, Mrs. B," I began, "then who did?"

From behind us came a quick "*Ahem.*"

"We did."

Akiko, Mae, and I spun around. Two women were

standing there. Their figures were framed by a bright red door behind them. One wore a radio headset draped around her neck, and the other hugged a notebook to her chest.

"We're sorry, Mrs. B," began the older woman, shifting the notebook to her hip. "We had to call them. Genevieve and I, well . . . we understand your worry about risks. And we know you'd never want to put these girls in so much danger. But—"

"But we must use everything we have for this mission," said the younger one. "And that means the Infinity Trinity."

Akiko's hand was on my shoulder, and she gave it such a squeeze, I thought my arm might snap off. Mae was on the other side of me, and I could hear gasp.

"You mean to say," I began, trying to get my brain to catch up with what was happening right before our eyes, "that you know who we are?"

"Nobody's supposed to know our real identities," whispered Mae. Her face looked stricken.

"And who are you?" asked Akiko. "We've never seen you before."

Mrs. B let out a deep, exasperated sigh. Then, fixing her fierce eyes on the two women, she said something about the league of secret heroes and protecting its members. "There's a reason the message you found in Japantown was so clever," she said tightly. "Because you're looking at two of the finest cryptologists of the war."

"*Cryptologists?*" piped up Mae, eager and excited.

"The study of pyramids?" I whispered to Akiko, a little unsure. "And mummies?"

"You and the mummies," Akiko said, slapping her hand to her forehead. "Not crypts and mummies. Cryptology is the study of codes—like writing them and solving them."

I really wished her whispers were quieter.

"Mae, Josie, Akiko," announced Mrs. B, "meet Elizebeth Friedman." She crossed the room to stand between the two women, nodding toward the older one. "Elizebeth is one of the best code crackers Room Twelve has ever known."

A code cracker? My eyes took in every detail. Elizebeth wasn't much taller than the three of us, with dark hair, arching eyebrows, and sharp eyes. Her smile was the kind I liked—quick and welcoming, not some forced thing people sometimes pasted to their lips.

"She got her start at Chicago's Newberry Library, like your grandmother, Mae," continued Mrs. B, her voice still tight but sounding less annoyed than a few minutes ago. "Elizebeth was asked to use her deep knowledge of Shakespeare to crack his sonnets—to prove they were written by someone other than Mr. Shakespeare himself. During the Great War, she became an expert in cryptology, solving tens of thousands of secret messages.

"And now, with this war, Elizebeth has become a master. We're lucky she's part of our league of secret heroes."

I was so stunned, I couldn't find my voice. It had grown feet and run off, leaving me standing there empty. Akiko was surprisingly speechless too, for someone who always seemed to have an opinion about everything.

"We're pleased to meet you," said Mae. And she did one of those handshakes that comes with a quick nod and a half curtsy. Akiko and I followed her lead.

Mrs. B turned to the younger woman next.

"And, girls, this is Genevieve Grotjan. Genevieve is a mathematician like your cousin Kay McNulty, Josie." Mrs. B waited for us to do another round of nodding and hand shaking and half curtsying before she went on. "Genevieve is another excellent code cracker."

She was taller than Elizebeth, and her hair was shorter with soft curls that framed her face. Her expression was almost sweet, despite all the tension in the air.

"We're puzzle solvers too," Mae said softly. "If you don't mind us asking, what kind of code cracking are you doing for Room Twelve?"

"That's a good question," Genevieve said, fiddling with the cord on her headset. "You have likely learned about the Enigma machine used by the Nazi military to encode messages in Europe? Our counterparts over in England— in Bletchley Park—are working around the clock to crack those German codes.

"Well, right here, looking west to the Japanese military,

we are working nonstop to crack Purple. That's the name given to Japan's cipher machine."

Mrs. B folded her arms over her chest, then gave a nod to Genevieve and Elizebeth on either side of her.

"We have the excellent minds of Genevieve and Elizebeth," Mrs. B began. I could see lines of worry etched in her face. "But there is tremendous danger afoot here in San Francisco. A powerful criminal called Side-Splitter seems to be working with the enemy to intercept secret codes. I suspect that's why—"

"That is precisely why," interrupted Elizebeth, "we summoned you. We need as much power as possible to bring this villain down."

Genevieve looked from Mrs. B to Elizebeth to us.

"We'd heard about your fight against the Hisser in Philadelphia," she said gently. "So we hoped to reach you with our message, inviting you here. But before meeting you now, we did not know your real identities. Only that Mrs. B wanted to protect you from such overwhelming evil.

"But now, more than ever, our league of secret heroes needs you."

"We know the danger," Akiko said. "We've already met Side-Splitter."

When she heard this, Mrs. B's eyes flickered.

"We're so sorry," Elizebeth began. "We wanted to warn you first."

"We have been trying to stay one step ahead of him," Genevieve said. "But Side-Splitter has been able to disrupt our radio transmissions, and he's solving coded messages faster than we can. The danger grows bigger every day."

Secrets? Codes? At the sound of those words, the three of us perked up.

"To beat Side-Splitter," continued Mrs. B, "we have to shut down his powers. We have to take away his ability to intercept important messages, as well as his power to pass along valuable information to Hitler and his army, not to mention call for attacks from the Japanese military."

"The balloon bombs!" I shouted. "He's behind them."

"That's right, and who knows what other kinds of weapons he's willing to unleash." Mrs. B paused, staring hard at the three of us. "You've already risked so much for Room Twelve. What we ask of you now is tremendous, and I had feared it was too much. Selfishly, it is for my sister's sake—"

"No, not only for Zenobia," interrupted Elizabeth, shaking her head. "It is Zenobia we'd like to save, of course. But now it's become larger than that. The stakes, I'm sorry to say, are nothing less than the fate of the free world."

Seventeen

*G*ULP.

I felt Mae's elbow in my rib cage. And on the other side of me, I could hear Akiko's raspy breathing grow even louder than it usually was. *We're just kids*, I wanted to say. *How can anybody count on us to save the world?*

Elizebeth led us toward her desk in the far corner of the room. It was heavy and wooden, like important things happened there. Folders and papers were piled high, and I counted at least three telephones. Just as she turned to speak to us, someone opened the red door and called out Genevieve's name.

"We need you," shouted a man wearing a headset similar

to Genevieve's. His hand was cupped to his mouth as he tried to be heard over the busy hum of activity. Peering into the room behind him, I could see a bank of radios and people working at tables. "There's a lot of chatter on the wires happening right now! Come on!"

"I've got to get back," Genevieve said, looking torn between staying with us and dashing off to the radio room. "But please know how grateful Elizebeth and I are that you're here. Code cracking is our lives right now. And if we can add power to our efforts, well . . ."

She looked at Elizebeth, who seemed to agree with whatever Genevieve was leaving unspoken.

"What Genevieve means is, a single star may shine brightly," Elizebeth said, "but a constellation of stars can light the way."

Genevieve excused herself and disappeared through the red door. I wondered what she would hear when she pulled her headset over her ears and listened in on one of those radios.

Elizebeth set her notebook down on her desk and drew our attention back to her.

"The three of you have shown great puzzling ability," she began, opening to a page she'd marked with a long ribbon. "Perhaps you might take an interest in the work we have before us today. It's the case of a San Francisco business owner who we suspect might be sending secret codes to help the enemy."

Elizebeth thumbed through a few pages, then set a series of yellowed papers on her desk. Akiko, Mae, and I leaned in for a closer look. They were letters typed on crisp stationery.

"We believe these messages are written in open code," she explained, "meaning the secrets are right in front of us, in the open. The letters are chatty, and nothing is meant to arouse suspicion. This isn't the typical case I crack, you see, yet it's a fascinating one."

Mae began reading one of the letters, her eyes moving quickly. "He's talking about dolls here. How are dolls suspicious?"

"He misspelled the word 'destroyed' here," said Akiko, tapping the page.

"And in that same sentence, he says something about a Mr. Shaw." I was leaning over Akiko's and Mae's shoulders in order to see. "Do you know who Mr. Shaw is? The letter writer says he was sick but is going back to work soon. Where does Mr. Shaw work?"

Elizebeth flashed a smile and shot an approving look at Mrs. B.

"You've pulled out crucial information," she said. "And I will tell you more so you see what we're dealing with:

"The USS *Shaw* is a navy ship—a destroyer—that was damaged in the attack on Pearl Harbor," Elizebeth explained. "We believe our suspect was reporting on its repair and when it would return to sea after being docked here on the West Coast."

Akiko, Mae, and I jumped to the next letters, hungry to read more.

"But he's mentioning dolls in all of these letters," Akiko said. "Dolls don't exactly have a lot to do with war. Why does he do that?"

Elizebeth and Mrs. B both nodded.

"*He* is actually a *she*. And that's our nickname for her," Elizebeth explained. "We call her the Doll Lady. You see, our suspect runs an antiques shop that specializes in dolls and toys. It's located in Japantown—"

"Hey, we know that store," began Mae. But Akiko stepped on her toe and gave a quick shake of her head, signaling for Mae to be quiet.

Were they talking about the toy shop in Akiko's neighborhood? Across from her dad's old dentist office?

Mrs. B said something about the suspect being a member of the Japanese-American Society, making regular visits to the Japanese consulate, socializing with high-ranking Japanese government officials, even entertaining them in her home.

"Just because you socialize with someone doesn't make you a spy," Akiko said hoarsely.

"Excellent point, Akiko," Elizebeth said. "Good code crackers exercise caution and rely on sound evidence. That is why we're continuing to study the case. We need more to go on than this."

She pulled out a few more documents from her notebook—crinkly papers and a few photographs—and spread them on the desk.

"Operatives from Room Twelve have been following the Doll Lady's movements around the city," Elizabeth went on. "We are tracking her messages with the Japanese Navy, and we're monitoring her work with our biggest nemesis, Side-Splitter."

As Elizabeth turned the black-and-white photographs toward us, Mae, Akiko, and I leaned in closer, resting our elbows on the desktop to take them in. One photo featured a woman in a wide hat crossing the street. Another was of a woman shopping at a fruit market. Another was a woman walking into what looked like that same doll shop we'd seen in Akiko's neighborhood.

"That's her?" I asked, straightening one of the pictures. The Doll Lady had pale skin and wavy hair that might have been blond or light brown. She wore it tied back in a bun. In each photograph she was wearing a wide, flat hat, which was the latest style. "She looks like anyone you'd see on the street, not somebody who's working with the enemy!"

"Yes, these are the latest pictures we have of the Doll Lady," Mrs. B said. "Her real name is Velvalee Dickinson."

Beside me, Akiko's knees seemed to give out.

Elizebeth had set out three more photographs. They featured the Doll Lady, but at her side was another figure. This woman had dark hair, bright eyes, and her face wore an expression that looked a lot like Akiko's.

"My mom," Akiko whispered. This time her voice was so soft, I wondered whether I'd imagined it.

"Are you okay?" asked Mrs. B, reaching over the desk and cupping Akiko's cheek. "You look as if you're going to be ill."

"H-her mom," I began, unsure of what to do or say. I wrapped an arm under her shoulder and tried to hold her up. "Akiko . . ."

"Akiko and her mom have allergies," Mae finished, lifting up Akiko's other side. "She just needs to sit down."

Eighteen

WE SLEPT FOR THE NIGHT IN ANOTHER room, all the way at the far end of the hall. Bunk beds lined the walls, and we saw a few familiar faces from Room Twelve coming and going into a similar arrangement across from us. These code-cracking teams really did seem to work around the clock, catching only a few hours' sleep when they could and getting back to work at a moment's notice.

"The Doll Lady." Those were Akiko's first words when we woke in the morning. Although she didn't exactly speak them—it was more like a groan. The springs above me creaked as she rolled over. "And my mom."

"How can it be true?" asked Mae, who was sleeping in

the top bed on the bunk beside ours. "A toy seller passing secrets to the enemy? It sounds like the plot of a mystery novel my granny would read."

"And your mom being involved somehow, Akiko?" I said. My bunk creaked even more than Akiko's when I sat up and put my feet on the floor. "Clearly there's some kind of misunderstanding."

Akiko dangled her legs off her mattress. She sounded confused as she tried to make sense of what we'd heard from Mrs. B and that code cracker, Elizebeth Friedman. "Maybe it was all just a coincidence," she said. "Maybe Velvalee, the one they're calling the Doll Lady, really did have a friend named Mr. Shaw who had been sick. And he just happened to have the same name as that USS *Shaw* destroyer ship that had been damaged and repaired."

Mae was silent. I stood between our bunks now and gave her a questioning look. I didn't want to think bad things about Akiko's mom any more than she—or Akiko—did.

"Let's take this stitch by stitch, the way my cousin Kay always says to do things," I said. "We can't jump to conclusions about your mom, Akiko. So let's break this down one step at a time."

Mae hopped off her bunk now too. Always sunny, always ready to think the best of people, she gave a quick tug on Akiko's dangling toes.

"Elizebeth is supposed to be the best code cracker in

America," Mae told her. "Remember what she said last night? Something about three important ships being repaired right now—an aircraft carrier, a battleship, and a destroyer. Let's get down to the shipyard and see for ourselves what's in dock. Maybe we'll find something that puts our minds at ease about your mom."

Akiko brightened a little at the idea of solving this mystery ourselves. But just as she jumped off the top bunk, an explosion rang out.

Ka-boom!

We raced out the door of the sleeping quarters and back into Room Twelve, tucking our shirts into our pants and skirts as we ran. None of us had packed bags for this journey, so we'd just slept in our clothes last night. I was fine with it, but I suspected tidy Mae wasn't going to approve of another night without real pajamas.

Before we could get any words out to offer our help, Mrs. B was on her feet and pacing.

"This is exactly what I wanted to avoid," she said with a nod toward the window. "It seems Side-Splitter is a little upset this morning about being challenged by a trio of superheroes. *Girls*, he complained. So he's rolling a few of his dangerous cannonballs down Lombard Street."

I asked what Lombard Street was. Should we head over there and protect it?

Elizebeth appeared beside Mrs. B, gulping a cup of coffee and poking a pencil behind her ear. "Lombard Street is the crookedest street in the world," she explained. "It zigs and zags down a steep hill, so his deadly cannonballs pick up speed as they roll from top to bottom."

"And at the bottom of the street is a navy outpost." Mrs. B sighed. "It's empty, as the officers have moved to a different location. But Side-Splitter didn't know that. He's outraged and, like any toddler who didn't get his way, is lashing out."

Both Mrs. B and Elizebeth recommended we keep our distance from Side-Splitter today, at least until they gathered more information. "We'll update you as soon as possible," Mrs. B assured us. "But until then, I'd feel more comfortable knowing you were ready for anything that might come your way. So I have a bit of homework you can do."

Homework? During summer vacation?

Akiko, Mae, and I were just starting to protest when a shout interrupted us, and the red door swung open.

"I—I think I've got something!"

It was Genevieve. She was breathless as she dashed over to a desk where a few other code crackers were seated. The man at the center was her boss, it seemed.

Genevieve laid out a stack of papers and showed them whatever she was working on. The group huddled around her as she ran her pencil under the figures. Mae, Akiko, and I crowded in too, and Mrs. B stood with Elizebeth at the edge of the group. Genevieve pointed out her pencil marks— she'd circled a place where two letters came together, then another two letters, and another, and another. Everyone around us seemed to be holding their breath in suspense, trying to make sense of what she'd discovered.

"This is it!" shouted one of the men. "Genevieve's cracked it!"

"Purple?" hollered someone else. "Genevieve's cracked Purple?"

"She has." The one who seemed like her boss sighed, taking off his glasses and flopping back into his chair as if he'd run a marathon. "Genevieve has done it."

Whooping and cheering suddenly filled Room Twelve. Mrs. B leaned over and filled us in on the reason behind the wild celebrating.

"We've been at this for more than a year," she said. "Purple is the machine the Japanese military uses to encrypt communication with their diplomats around the world. Now, it seems, we will have a window into those secret messages."

Genevieve's cheeks were flushed with excitement and maybe even a little embarrassment by all the attention. "I noticed a pattern within a pattern," she said modestly. "It's what we do as puzzler solvers."

Akiko, Mae, and I were nearly as excited as the other code crackers. Because we looked for patterns when we solved puzzles too. I could hardly imagine cracking a code as important as the one Genevieve just solved.

"This could change the direction of the whole war," one of the puzzlers said. "Think of all the information we can learn—about where enemy ships plan to attack or when enemy bombers plan to fly."

"It might save a lot of lives," said another.

Immediately my heart clenched as I thought about my dad. And Mam. And everyone else who lost someone they loved in this terrible war. I noticed Mrs. B look downward and squeeze her eyes shut. She was probably thinking about her sister Zenobia.

Akiko reached over and gave my hand a squeeze.

"Like my brother Tommy's life," she whispered. And turning to Mae, she took her hand too.

"And my daddy's too," Mae said softly.

No matter what we did, the people we loved most in the world were never far from our thoughts.

"Let's celebrate," said Mrs. B with a smile. "Coca-Colas for everyone!"

Nineteen

ONCE THE EXCITEMENT OVER CRACKING Purple died down, Mrs. B and Elizebeth led us to a long wooden table on the other side of the room, not far from Elizebeth's big desk. Three headsets were plugged into a radio, and pencils and paper were piled in the middle.

"We've picked up a faint signal," Elizebeth explained, her eyes flashing as she looked from Akiko to Mae to me. "We could use your help right away. There's reason to believe it is coming from one of our operatives who has gone missing. This is of crucial importance."

Mrs. B looked equally concerned. Where she was tall and stood ramrod straight, Elizebeth was shorter, her movements quicker. But their minds seemed to run at the same lightning speed.

"We've taken the liberty to set the three of you up here," Mrs. B said, twisting the dial on the radio and pressing one of the headsets to her left ear. "We'd like you to record whatever you can pick up, then try to make sense of it. Listen for Morse code, for patterns or substitutions. Use whatever powers of puzzling you can."

Akiko took a seat at the head of the table. I plunked down on her left and Mae to her right. Once Mrs. B and Elizebeth disappeared, we leaned in to whisper.

"What do you think?" wondered Akiko as she wrestled with the bulky headset. "Will these messages be coming from the Pacific? From some lost sailors adrift in a submarine?"

"Or they could come from Germany. Or even France," said Mae, resting her headset at her neck like a scarf. "I'll do whatever it takes to make sure my daddy is safe."

"It could come from anywhere," I said, pulling at the cord as it tangled in my hair. "From land, sea, even from the air. What if it's a bomber pilot wanting tips to find his target?"

Whatever it was, we were eager to help. Grabbing pencils and notepads, we gave a nod to Akiko as she reached for the radio and turned up the volume.

Crackles and zips sounded in my ears. I fiddled with

the rainbow-shaped headband, then pressed the rubber cups more snuggly over my ears. Again, my head was filled with the sounds of popping and crackling. Mae pointed at the headset over her ears and shook her head. Akiko sat motionless, her mouth hanging open just a bit as she concentrated.

Nothing. Just noisy static.

Then a rumbling sound suddenly filled my headphones. It reminded me of a car engine. And a man's voice came through, but I couldn't quite pin it down.

"Is that French?" exclaimed Akiko.

"It's not English," said Mae. "Wait, there's something else."

I heard a woman's voice, higher-pitched and cleaner, start to edge out the man's words.

"I think that one's German," I said. "It reminds me of Gerda at the diner. *Guten Morgen*—Gerda taught me that. It means 'good morning.'"

More static, more popping, more voices coming and going in unfamiliar languages. I even caught a faint stream of music, high and tinny like a violin.

Then something else.

Mae's hands shot to her ears as she strained to catch this new voice. Akiko leaned even closer into the table, her nose nearly touching her notepad. I sat perfectly still, afraid that if I moved, it would disappear.

"Sun or shine! Sun or shine . . ."

This voice was in English. It sounded as if a woman were speaking.

Static interrupted her words, like someone was wadding up a ball of paper right beside my ear.

"Sun or shine," came the voice again. I grabbed my pencil and began to write.

"Catch all persons entering Denver, Houston. Exiting Reno or East Seattle. Interrogate next day. At night gather every radio. Sun or shine. Sun or shine."

Then static again. A few fizzy bursts followed until the report went silent.

"Seattle," said Akiko, her breath raspy as she rushed to finish scribbling down the message. With her other hand, she tugged her headset off her ears and let it hang around her neck. "'Seattle' has two *T*s. And 'interrogate' has two *R*s."

"Like Genevieve with the Purple code?" said Mae, tucking her legs beneath her and sitting up higher in her chair. "You're looking at patterns? I'm looking at the actual words. Is there a battleship called the *Denver*? Or the *Reno*? Are there ports in Seattle and Houston? What if they're being targeted for attack?"

"She said 'at night,' something about 'gathering every radio,'" I said, running a pencil under the words I'd jotted down. "Does that mean a nighttime attack?"

It went on like this for the rest of the morning. Akiko

would think she was onto something, and then Mae would throw in another idea, and I would add another. Then the first solution would collapse under the weight of it all.

"This doesn't make sense," complained Akiko, pulling a piece of bubble gum out of her Hauntima bag as she stared at her notebook. She passed pieces to Mae and me. My stomach rumbled, and I couldn't help but wonder if Akiko could produce a chocolate malted or a slice of pie if I asked.

"Of course it doesn't make sense," said Mae, her voice still smooth and sunny despite her frustration. "It's most likely a coded message and not some ordinary radio news report."

"And that's the thing," I said, heading off any bickering between the two of them. "We have to write down all these words and see what's ordinary news and what's not."

But Akiko wasn't satisfied. She adjusted her barrette and huffed. "No, I'm talking about this expression—*sun or shine*—it doesn't make any sense. You'd say 'rain or shine,' or 'sun or shade.' But as it is, 'sun or shine' is the same thing: sunny."

I wrote the phrase again in my notebook.

I could feel their eyes following my pencil as it scratched across the paper.

"That's it!" Mae shouted, her finger shooting at my paper like a dart. "The first letters of *sun or shine*! S-O-S!"

She was right! It stood out like a flashlight in the darkness.

"Write out the next part," Akiko croaked, pushing at my arm.

I took a deep breath to steady my hand, and I began to write the message again.

CATCH ALL PERSONS ENTERING
DENVER, HOUSTON.
EXITING RENO OR EAST SEATTLE.
INTERROGATE NEXT DAY.
AT NIGHT GATHER EVERY RADIO.

All three of us were pressed in close, studying every up and down of my pencil. And it wasn't just Akiko's breathing that was noisy. Mae and I were practically panting as we deciphered the clues too, piecing together new words from the first letter of every one we saw here.

"'Catch all persons'—C-A-P. That's spells 'CAP'!" I said.

"No, 'catch all persons entering'—that's C-A-P-E, CAPE!" corrected Akiko.

"Add 'Denver,'" said Mae, nearly shouting. "'Catch all persons entering Denver'—that spells CAPED!"

We jumped to the next words.

"'Houston,'" I said, my voice tense with excitement. "'Exiting Reno or East Seattle. H-E-R-O-E-S.' That spells out 'HEROES.'"

"I see D-A-N, DAN," said Akiko, clutching Mae's

arm as she tried to solve the next clues. "Who do you think Dan is?"

"You jumped ahead," Mae pointed out. And taking her time, she tapped each word on my page. "'Interrogate next day. At night gather every radio.' That's not *DAN*, that's *I-N* and then *D-A-N-G-E-R*. 'IN DANGER'!"

My eyes flashed across the page as I frantically tried to solve the whole puzzle:

SUN OR SHINE.
CATCH ALL PERSONS ENTERING
DENVER, HOUSTON.
EXITING RENO OR EAST SEATTLE.
INTERROGATE NEXT DAY.
AT NIGHT GATHER EVERY RADIO.
SUN OR SHINE.

"S-O-S," I heaved, barely getting the words out as panic seized my chest. "Caped heroes in danger."

And together, our voices heavy, we repeated that urgent distress call, known around the world. "S-O-S."

Twenty

AKIKO JUMPED TO HER FEET AND WAVED for Elizebeth to come over.

"We heard a message and cracked it!" Her voice was steady despite her pink cheeks and raspy breath. "Just like Genevieve! We figured out the code, and we deciphered it."

"It was an acrostic puzzle," Mae explained. "The first letter of every word spelled out a distress call."

"At first pass, it seemed like a simple message," I added. "But there's so much more being said! Superheroes are in danger! They need help now!"

Elizebeth maintained her cool, calm manner as she

whispered in an assistant's ear. Moments later Mrs. B appeared, her face tense.

"What did you learn, girls?" she asked quickly.

"Distress call," explained Elizebeth, passing along my notebook. "What we don't know is the source of the message. It could be coming from anywhere on the globe. An island in the Pacific, from Russia, someplace in Europe, even from here in the United States."

Mrs. B set the paper down and nodded toward our equipment.

"Did the sender identify themselves in any way?" There was a sadness in her eyes that I knew must have something to do with her missing sister. To Mrs. B, Zenobia was more than the world's most important superhero. She was family. "Did they mention a geographical landmark that could be a clue to their location? A song or book that might be a signal to us?"

Mae pulled her headset back on. "We'll stay on it, Mrs. B, until we find out."

Akiko and I moved back toward our chairs too, but we were filled with questions.

"Hopscotch helped us yesterday," I began. "On our way here, trying to find Room Twelve. She appeared when we battled with Side-Splitter—"

"But she was like a ghost," Akiko interrupted. "It was the same with Hauntima, too. Why are they just shadows of themselves? What's happening to them?"

"Why are their powers fading?" I added. "Both Hopscotch and Hauntima seemed so drained of energy."

Astra crossed the room toward our table, then curled up on the floor near Mrs. B's feet. She reached down and rubbed his eyebrows.

Just as she straightened up, Mae called out from the radio.

"I've got something else," she shouted. "It's in Morse code, I think!"

Mae's pencil glided across the page, line upon line, as Akiko and I jumped into our seats beside her. We tugged on our headsets too.

"'Get the wee three,'" Mae began, quickly decoding the phrase she'd recorded. "'Only a few more left. No more clowning around.'"

"There's that nickname again," croaked Akiko. "It's kind of annoying that people don't call us—"

Now it was my turn to interrupt.

"*Wee three?*" I said, feeling outrage start to bubble up from the pit of my stomach. "Are they talking about coming after us?"

Mrs. B signaled for Akiko and me to be quiet. She wanted to hear more of Mae's message as she translated the Morse code. "This is most likely Side-Splitter," she explained. "He's contacting his network about the next step. This is deadly serious."

Mae read off more of the message she'd picked up.

"He's saying: 'Caped crybabies must be stopped,'" she said. Her eyes shot to Mrs. B's face for a split second, then back down to the page. "The final phrase," and here Mae hesitated, lifting her pencil and staring in shock at what she'd just translated from the jumble of dashes and dots of the Morse code. Her voice was flat but tinged with a hint of fear.

"'Eliminate hopper, hound, and horse.'"

Suddenly the lights flickered in the room, and the whole building seemed to let out a moan. The radio fizzled off, and when someone near a window peeked outside, the sky seemed to have gone dark. What was Side-Splitter doing? With powers like his, could he sap all the electricity out of San Francisco? Then with a crack, the radio fired back to life and the day was bright again.

I shuddered.

Elizebeth stood over Mae's shoulder, double-checking her translation of Side-Splitter's message. When she finished, she gave a quick nod to Mrs. B that Mae was correct. "Dreadful," she whispered.

"Who's next?" croaked Akiko. "He's coming back for the Infinity Trinity and hopper—"

Akiko's thoughts seemed to interrupt her speech as she came to the same realization as the rest of us. "That's got to be Hopscotch!"

And then it hit me. When he said 'hound and horse,' Side-Splitter could mean only one thing: Star and the Palomino.

"As with the Hisser in Philadelphia," said Mrs. B, her eyes on Astra's sleeping form, "Side-Splitter is familiar to us. Hopscotch, Zenobia, Star, and I had a run-in with him years ago. And you could say it was . . . well, unpleasant. It seems he is out for revenge."

I tried to swallow, but it was hard to make the lump in my throat disappear. Side-Splitter was a maniacal menace. From just our one encounter, it was clear that he was unpredictable and cruel. And not a fan of superheroes of any kind.

"He's coming for us now," I whispered. "Because—"

"Because he's already gotten to Zenobia and the others," added Akiko.

The room went silent.

"Is he the reason why Hopscotch and Hauntima are weaker?" asked Mae. "Is he draining their strength too?"

Mrs. B's expression was stony, but I thought I saw her flinch.

Though my mind was clouded with questions, one thing shone perfectly clear. The path to finding Zenobia led in one direction. And that was through Side-Splitter.

Twenty-One

WE NEED TO CONSULT WITH GENEVIEVE about these messages," Mrs. B said. "Please excuse Elizebeth and me for a few hours. I don't want to alarm you unnecessarily. So I ask for your patience."

Elizebeth gave us a courteous nod as she followed Mrs. B, but Astra barely lifted his head from his napping spot. I could hear him faintly snoring. Mrs. B pulled the red door shut behind her with a firm *click*.

We stood still for a few moments, staring at the door.

"We can't just wait around," Akiko said finally. "Let's get out of here."

"But we've got to stay safe," I said. Mam's warning

echoed in my mind. How could I take such risks when I knew how much she was already hurting?

Mae gave my hand a squeeze. "Side-Splitter knows the Infinity Trinity, but he doesn't know Josie, Akiko, and Mae. We'll be okay."

We were down the staircase moments later and pushing through the Ferry Building's front doors. We decided to make our way along the waterfront, like yesterday. The Bay Bridge rose like a steel mountain ahead of us, its twisting cables and majestic towers soaring into the sky. There were a few burnt-looking patches marking up the metal, where Side-Splitter's attacks must have hit. But otherwise it was intact and busy with cars coming and going.

Horns honked and seagulls called, but my favorite noise was the barking of the sea lions that heaved their massive bodies out of the water to sun themselves on every available pier, boat, and dinghy. They reminded me of sandbags with flippers. And they smelled even worse than they sounded. Mae was in love.

"Look at those big brown eyes," she cooed. "They're sleepy but intelligent."

After a few blocks, Akiko let out a shout. I was waiting for her to complain about the stinking sea lions and about Mae giving names to the noisiest ones. But instead she was hollering about breakfast—or this late in the day, lunch.

"I spy pie!" she announced. And grabbing Mae and me

each by an elbow, she led us across the street toward a tiny redbrick diner with a flashing neon sign. My mouth started watering before we'd even scooted into a booth.

"Sorry. We're out of pie," announced the waitress. "But we've got pudding."

We settled on buttered toast and Dr Pepper before turning our talk to the cracked codes and threatening messages. So much had already happened, and we hadn't even been in San Francisco for more than a day.

"When Mrs. B warned us about the Hisser's deadly gaze back in Philadelphia," began Mae, "it was because she'd met him in battle. She knew his tricks."

"Right," I agreed. "And she knows about Side-Splitter, too. We'll have to ask her what to look for in case we have another run-in with him."

"Of course we'll have another run-in with Side-Splitter," said Akiko, nearly spilling her soda. "He just announced he's coming for all of us!"

Mae and I hushed Akiko and her whisper-shouts. We didn't need anyone listening in on our conversation.

"This is feeling a little overwhelming," Mae said, rubbing her fingers to her temples. "Let's break it down into manageable parts."

"What part of 'deranged clown' is manageable?" asked Akiko, her eyes bugging.

"Mae's right," I said, trying to head off their usual

back-and-forth. "Let's go over it stitch by stitch. Then we can solve it."

Akiko slathered a little more butter on her toast, appearing unconvinced.

"First there was the S-O-S message," I said. "Whoever is sending it is in danger. We've got to find them."

"Right, but how? Where are they?" asked Mae. "I listened to the tapping of that Morse code message. It was faint, like a phantom message."

"Just like Hauntima and Hopscotch," added Akiko. "They're ghosts now."

The waitress refilled our Dr Peppers and brought three more slices of toast, this time with strawberry jam. We stopped our talking, not only because we didn't want her listening in on our conversation. But mostly because the aroma of warm fruit was overpowering. I ate almost half my toast before looking back up at Akiko and Mae across from me.

"How powerful do you think Side-Splitter is?" Mae asked, dabbing at the corners of her mouth.

"You saw how tense Mrs. B looked, and Elizebeth and Genevieve, too," Akiko said. "They have plenty to do battling the Nazis and the Japanese military. Then add in fighting with a maniacal clown? How can they do it all?"

I fiddled with my straw, poking at an ice cube as my mind tried to work through all the details. So many people were in danger—from ordinary tourists all the way to superheroes like Zenobia, Hopscotch, the Palomino, and even Star.

Thoughts simmered in my mind like a stew. But I kept coming back to the same worry. And it was almost too much to speak.

I stared at Akiko and Mae, trying to find my voice.

"Wh-what if . . . ?" I began. Goose bumps broke out on my arms and shimmied up my whole body. "What if they're working together?"

"Who?" asked Mae.

I shifted uncomfortably in the booth. "The Hisser, Side-Splitter, and the other vil—"

But before I got any further, Akiko spilled her soda. Her hand trembled as she pointed out the window.

"There they are!" she heaved, finger tapping the glass. "My mom! And the Doll Lady! They're walking along the waterfront near the ships. Right there—in the pink cartwheel hat."

"What's a cartwheel hat?" I exclaimed in the quietest shout I could manage. I wasn't exactly the kind to stay up to date on the latest fashions. "I have no idea what I'm looking for!"

"It's a hat the size of a wheel," Mae said quickly and gently, her eyes scanning the crowd. "But I think of them like an oversize pancake balanced on the head."

Mae and I pressed against the window for a better

view as Akiko directed our eyes down the road. I caught sight of what had to be the woman they were talking about. Her pink hat was round and flat, and her jacket was pink too.

I couldn't see her face, but Akiko was certain it was Velvalee Dickinson.

"And beside her, in the green beret with the little bow on top," she said, her usual gravelly voice sounding heavy with worry. "I'd know that beret anywhere. We gave it to Mom for Mother's Day a couple years ago."

Akiko went silent. Her face paled as she stared out the window, probably wondering what was going through her mom's mind right now. Was she in danger? To be working side by side with the Doll Lady, had someone threatened her? Threatened Akiko's family?

"What if someone is making her do this?" I asked. "You know, forcing her."

Mae set down her toast, slid out of the booth, and got to her feet.

"Shake a leg, you two," she said. "We have to do one of the hardest things of our lives right now. Harder than punching a giant rattlesnake in the nose. More difficult than beating back a demonic clown."

I scooted out from my side of the booth and looked at them. Akiko kept her eyes fixed out the window, her fingers fiddling with the strap of her Hauntima bag.

"What, Mae?" I asked. "What's the hardest thing?"

She reached over and laid her hand gently on Akiko's shoulder. Her voice was soft as she spoke, leaning closer to Akiko and me. "We have to find out whether someone we love is in danger."

Twenty-Two

BY THE TIME WE GOT TO THE WATERFRONT, the Doll Lady and Akiko's mom were already blocks ahead of us. We tried not to attract attention by running, so the three of us set out walking at a quick pace, as if we were late for a meeting.

It didn't take long to spot the two familiar hats up just ahead of us. Velvalee was tossing what must have been bread crusts toward the water's edge, and seagulls and other birds fought to gobble up the treats. Akiko's mom stood nearby with a pencil and paper, looking as if she were sketching the birds.

"What are they doing?" I asked. "Do you think they're

going to tie a note to a bird's leg and send a message? Like they do with homing pigeons?"

"That would be clever," whispered Mae. "Room Twelve thinks the Doll Lady is sharing secrets with the Japanese military. But wouldn't a pigeon get tired flying across the entire Pacific Ocean to Japan?"

"Then how do you think she's transmitting the information?" Akiko asked. She reached into her bag and pulled out a hankie. When she blew her nose, it was almost as loud as one of the passing ships' horns. I couldn't help but notice her mom turn around, like she was searching the crowd. Had she recognized Akiko's honking? Did she suspect we were there?

We ducked behind a stand of bicycles, just in case.

"Let's focus, like Hopscotch says," Mae said, sounding as if we were a couple of helpless first graders and not her brilliant, puzzle-solving, code-cracking partners. "Try to ignore the distractions and stay on task."

"We are," growled Akiko, pulling another piece of bubble gum out of her bag. She handed us each a piece, which gave us time to study the Doll Lady and Akiko's mom in quiet for a few moments. "We're trying to figure out what Velvalee Dickinson is up to. Maybe she's going to hand a message off to another spy."

"Or do a dead drop," I offered, "where they leave their note inside something, like bicycle handlebars or a hollowed-out rock in a park."

"We know what a dead drop is," said Mae, correcting without sounding like she was correcting. "Let's try to get in their minds, see things the way they are seeing it all."

Just beyond the Doll Lady's bread crumbs and the hungry birds, ships bobbed in the water. All kinds of navy vessels were docked up and down the piers throughout the bay, in fact, in plain view.

"Good idea, Mae," I said. "What exactly are they looking at?"

"Maybe that aircraft carrier," Akiko said as we strolled off to the right. We made sure to keep moving but still stay close enough to keep them in our sights. "What's hanging all over it? Seaweed? Or is that kelp?"

"That's netting," explained Mae. "I read about it in a military magazine when I was helping Granny Crumpler. Netting like that can protect ships from torpedoes and submarines."

Akiko nodded. But I could tell she was a little annoyed that Mae knew more ship trivia than she did.

We stood in silence, studying the crisscross pattern of the long nets. I wondered how much protection they could provide when an attack was happening. As I turned to ask Mae and Akiko what they thought, I glanced over my shoulder at where the Doll Lady and Akiko's mom had been standing. They were gone!

I rushed down the path in search of them. Akiko and Mae raced behind me.

"Slow down, Josie!" whispered Akiko. It was closer to a shout, so I eased my pace. The last thing we needed was Akiko's mom catching us.

"I see them," said Mae, trying to speak without moving her lips. And she pulled Akiko and me to her side and began pretending like we were tourists out for a bit of sight-seeing. She pointed this way and that, turning our bodies away from the waterfront. "We won't let them get away—they're directly over your shoulders, seated at a bench. The Doll Lady just pulled a doughnut from her bag, so they're snacking or something."

"I bet that's a signal for another spy to approach," Akiko said, her breathing raspy as she kept herself from turning around to check. "Do you see anyone talking with them?"

I craned my neck. Nobody was paying any attention to the Doll Lady or Akiko's mom. The crowds were thinner down here, along this part of the waterfront. The seagulls squawked, and a few pelicans perched on wooden posts. But otherwise there didn't seem to be other spies ready to meet with our suspects. Just some loud banging coming from one of the ships nearby.

"What's that noise?" I asked. I could see sailors with hammers. "Is somebody on the boat trying to give the Doll Lady a message? Is the hammering in Morse code?"

"It's a battleship, to be precise," Akiko announced. I saw her shoot a quick glance at Mae, and I knew she was making sure she scored points in this latest round of navy trivia. "I think those sailors over there are fixing the ship's deck. It's made of wood, so it must get pretty beat up while they're at sea."

We tried to look casual as we strolled along the pathway. We listened to the banging of the hammers blending with the squawking of the seagulls and the cranking of a tall crane that was moving equipment onto other ships docked nearby.

"It's clear from the letter Elizebeth showed us that the Doll Lady is spying," whispered Mae, her eyes lingering on their bench. "But your mom, Akiko. I don't know. Maybe she's just helping her with a new shipment of dolls. Maybe it's purely innocent, and she's not doing any sort of spying."

Akiko stared off toward the water. "That one there is called a destroyer," she said, almost as if she had too many facts in her brain and needed to release a few—like letting air out of a balloon. "Destroyers are smaller than those big boats. They're fast and nimble. Kind of like us."

Mae started to speak, but I jabbed her in the ribs. The Doll Lady and Akiko's mom were moving down the waterfront again. We couldn't let anything distract us.

"Pay attention, you two," I whispered. "She's up to something right now, and we can catch her in the act."

We looped arms and began walking again. The bright green beret that belonged to Akiko's mom bobbed along like a leaf in the flow of people ahead of us, and the Doll Lady's pink pancake hat stood out in the bright sunshine.

"I suspect the Doll Lady belongs to a complicated spy ring," Mae said. She was thinking out loud and nodding, as if she were agreeing with herself. "And that means a complicated way of communicating. She might use any number of spy tricks, like taking photos with a camera hidden in a matchbox."

"And don't forget mini submarines," added Akiko. "In one of my Hopscotch comic books, she battles a dangerous gang of spies that comes ashore from a mini sub."

We'd read enough comic books to know a long list of outrageous tricks the Doll Lady could use. "She might even be writing on a notebook that explodes if she gets caught," I warned. "Let's be ready for something big."

"Something flashy," agreed Mae.

"Something jaw-dropping," whisper-shouted Akiko.

As we rounded one of the curves along the waterfront, I drew up short as if my legs stopped working. Akiko let out a wheezy gasp, and Mae whispered a quick, "My stars!"

The Doll Lady was using a trick that hadn't even entered our minds.

A plain old, ordinary mailbox.

Twenty-Three

ALETTER?" SAID MAE, HER EYEBROWS shooting up. Akiko's mom and the Doll Lady quickly disappeared back into the San Francisco crowds, but Akiko, Mae, and I stood frozen in stunned silence. "We've got to get our hands on that letter before the mail carrier comes."

Akiko raced over to the mailbox. "Surely this thing must have a door you can open and shut." She ran her hands along the four sides of the mailbox, feeling for some sort of hinge or opening. Then she dropped onto the ground and tried to slide her body underneath for a peek.

"It's probably secured so you can't take mail out," I said, a little amazed at how agile Akiko was to inch herself under this big metal hunk. "The idea is that once you drop your letter in, you can trust that nobody comes along and pulls it out. Like we want to do."

Akiko got to her feet and adjusted her hair clip. She did not look ready for defeat.

"Okay, you two," she whispered. It was loud enough to attract the attention of a lonely seagull nearby, who cocked his head to one side and squawked at her. Looking first to the left, then right, she opened the mail slot and began slipping her skinny arm inside.

"Stop!" hollered Mae, and she grabbed Akiko's shoulder. "Tampering with the United States mail is a criminal offense! You told your little cousin yourself! Do you want to wind up on Alcatraz Island? With the rest of the criminals?"

"I know it is," huffed Akiko, pulling her arm back. "But I also don't want whatever's in that letter to reach any bad guys who want to do harm."

I tugged on the silver handle and tried to peer inside the mailbox. The long horizontal door creaked on its hinges, and all I could see was darkness. The seagull moved a little closer. Maybe it thought there were bread crumbs in there.

"This is the big question," I said, turning back to Akiko and Mae. "Do we choose to do something we know is wrong in order to help prevent something bad happening? Or do we choose to do nothing and know that by *not* acting, a terrible thing might occur?"

Mae appeared deep in thought, her eyes blinking a few times as she turned this over. Akiko let out a long puff of air and stared up at the gray clouds that were moving in. She chomped her bubble gum with a noisy smack, and I wondered if Mae would complain about ladylike manners.

"That's it, Akiko!" Mae's face looked as if she'd just won a spelling bee. "Gum!"

"What do you mean?" asked Akiko, clearly annoyed. "I've already given you two pieces."

"Yes," urged Mae impatiently. "And we need more! Now!"

Akiko dove her hands into her bag and rummaged frantically, like a squirrel looking for a nut. She pushed aside her umbrella, shoes, a comb. Before long, she emerged with three more pieces of bubble gum, one for each of us.

"Chew," Mae ordered. "Quickly!"

Akiko and I did as we were told. My jaw got a cramp from chomping so hard and so fast. I wondered if we looked like cows enjoying lunch.

"What are we doing?" Akiko managed to ask as she chewed. It came out sounding like "*Wha ah wa hooing?*"

But Mae didn't waste time trying to explain. She slapped her hunk of chewing gum into the middle of her palm, then gestured for us to do the same.

When the three wads of gum were piled together, Mae

balled them up like she was making a clay sculpture in art class. Then she began to roll and stretch the gum into a thick string. When it was nearly as long as my arm, she nodded to Akiko and me as if we knew exactly what she was thinking.

We stared at her, blinking.

"Go," Mae urged. "Open the mail slot."

Akiko and I tugged on the silver door. Just as it opened up, Mae plunked her sticky string inside, like she was dropping a fishing line into a pond. She tugged and dragged and angled the pink rope until, finally, she pulled up her catch.

I snatched it and looked around, half expecting a police officer to cuff me. The letter was addressed to a bank in Texas.

"I don't think that's it," whispered Mae, who looked so nervous her hands were shaking. "Again!"

We dropped the gum line into the mailbox again, then a third time and even a fourth. On the fifth try, we reeled in what seemed to be the right letter.

"Look at the return address." Mae gasped as the three of us leaned in close, nearly knocking our foreheads together. "That's it."

The letter was addressed to someone in Buenos Aires, Argentina. But the return address was what told us all we needed to know. It read *American Toy Company, 1744A Buchanan Street, San Francisco, California.*

"A toy company," I whispered as we passed the envelope to each other. "It sounds so innocent."

"But the Doll Lady," said Mae, her voice as serious as I'd ever heard her, "is definitely not playing around."

Twenty-Four

THE SEAGULL THAT HAD PERCHED SO CLOSE to us suddenly squawked again. Mae jumped and nearly dropped the letter from her hands. We needed to get somewhere quiet and read this without anyone noticing.

Akiko tucked the envelope into her bag, and we took off running toward a park across the street. I could see little kids splashing in a low fountain and couples sitting here and there on park benches. Accordion music drifted on the air, and a small monkey skittered around the musician and collected coins thrown from people strolling by.

We found a shady spot and sat down on the grass, nearly piling on top of each other as we caught our breath.

"Open it!" urged Mae.

"I thought tampering with mail was a criminal offense," teased Akiko, her hand clutching the letter.

"This is for the greater good!" snapped Mae impatiently. "Now open it!"

"But I don't want to break the seal," Akiko said. "How can we read it without tearing the envelope?"

I felt their eyes on me. Mae could pick locks, and Akiko was good at eavesdropping. It was my turn to show off my snooping skills.

"Hand me your barrette, Akiko," I said, putting out my hand.

She passed it over. Popping open the clasp, I slipped the flat metal edge into the lip of the envelope. Slowly, I wriggled it down the fold, inch by inch. I was careful not to tug too hard and tear the paper. Finally, I unsealed it.

"It looks as if all three of us would make pretty good spies," Mae said, nudging me with her shoulder.

"Eavesdropping is the best," Akiko pointed out. "They lock people in prison on Alcatraz Island for what you two have done picking locked doors and opening people's mail."

"Yes," I agreed, feeling a pang of guilt. "But right now intercepting this letter is much more important than whatever you overheard that cigar-smoking loudmouth saying in the hallway!"

We scooted closer together and pressed our heads in

tight, eager to see if we could make sense of what was written on the page. As Akiko ran her finger under the lines and read out loud, my heart pounded. It was as if we were touching a grenade that could explode at any moment.

> *"The only new dolls I have are three lovely Irish dolls. One of these three dolls is an old fisherman with a net over his back, another is an old woman with wood on her back, and the third is a little boy."*

In the letters Elizebeth had shown us earlier, the Doll Lady made things sound ordinary when what she really was writing about was the extraordinary. But this time there was no Mr. Shaw—neither a man nor a ship.

"Look at the first letter of each word," suggested Mae. "Did she write in code? Another acrostic spelling out her secret?"

We held our breath and read.

Nope.

"What about the first letter of each line?" I asked. "Does that spell anything?"

Nothing there, either.

"Let's rearrange some of the key words," Akiko said. "Maybe she's hidden her message that way."

But there were too many key words. Which ones would

she have used? Nothing was underlined or highlighted in any way.

"There has to be a secret in this, but what?" groaned Akiko. "She didn't have time for invisible ink. There aren't enough dashes and dots for there to be Morse code in here. No numbers for a book cipher. What can it be?"

We held the letter up toward the sun to see if there was anything hidden in the paper. Our eyes pored over Velvalee's writing again and again, line by line. Where was the secret? How had she hidden the message?

"Let's try this again," I said. "Maybe her secret is hiding in plain sight."

"Like your friend Emmett's laundry line," Mae said, nodding.

After a few more minutes of silence, Akiko pointed at one of the phrases. "What does she mean here? When she writes about 'an old fisherman with a net over his back'? We've seen fishermen up and down the waterfront. None of them looked particularly old to me."

Mae's eyes lit up. "But we did see a net! Do you remember when I told you about the netting on the aircraft carrier? How it protects from torpedoes and submarines?"

Akiko folded her arms across her chest and gave Mae an exasperated look. "Yes, we heard. You know all about torpedoes and netting."

"Mae, you're right!" I pointed toward those words in

the letter as I grabbed Akiko's arm. "This is a tip-off! The netting was on the aircraft carrier. The Doll Lady is telling somebody about that ship!"

Akiko's eyes flew back to the page again.

"Hauntima's ghost! Then this part where she talks about 'an old woman with wood on her back,'" she said, her words tumbling in a rush. "That could mean the battleship! We heard the hammering—repairing a *wooden* deck!"

Our heads cast shadows onto the paper, but nothing could slow down our reading. My finger raced to another phrase the Doll Lady had written.

"Here it is," I said, trying to keep from shouting in my excitement. "She says something about 'a little boy.' That's got to be the destroyer! You said so yourself, Akiko, that destroyer ships are small and nimble—like us!"

"And Elizabeth already told us to be on the lookout for three ships under repairs," Mae said, craning her neck toward the water and the enormous vessels we'd passed. "This is just the evidence we need to show what the Doll La—"

"Nosy Nellies!" shrieked a voice just behind us. And suddenly a white-gloved hand snatched the letter away. "You don't need to worry your little heads about this."

Akiko, Mae, and I scrambled to our feet and turned around. We were facing another street performer. It was the same one we'd seen playing the accordion, but there was something familiar about his hat and hair. He must have been one of Side-Splitter's copies! He passed the Doll Lady's letter to his pet monkey, who scampered up to sit on the man's shoulder. It began tearing the note into pieces.

"Give that back, you little beast," croaked Akiko. "That's ours!"

The clown slipped his sidekick a peanut and made no effort to retrieve our letter. His face wore a smile, but his eyes looked angry.

"It is not your letter," he snarled. "You stole it right out of that mailbox. So we stole it from you. *Monkey see, monkey do!* That's how the saying goes, right?"

And he burst into a laugh that made the hair on my arms stand straight up.

"We need that letter," Mae began, her hand reaching gently toward the monkey. "Come here, little pet. I won't hurt you."

But before she could get any closer, the clown began to play his accordion in a screeching wail. Suddenly another street performer rounded a corner toward us from the left. I turned and saw two more coming at us from the right. I figured they were all Side-Splitter's replicas, just waiting for his signal.

"Forget it," I hollered. "Let's get out of here while we still can!"

I plunged through the flowering bushes that lined the

park, and Mae and Akiko ran right behind me. We burst out of the greenery and onto the next block. But instead of losing the clowns, we seemed to be getting ourselves trapped. A burly one reached out and grabbed Akiko's arm just as she tried to slip past him.

"No!" shouted Mae as we held on to Akiko's waist. "Leave her alone!"

Just then a woman stepped between us and the clowns. Barely taller than we were, she didn't appear to be much of a threat to the figure who'd clamped on to Akiko's arm.

Suddenly, the woman swung her arm up and over. And as if it were happening in slow motion, we watched her flip the clown onto his back, flat as a pancake. Flat, even, as Velvalee Dickinson's hat!

"Take that!" she hollered. "The young lady said to stop!"

Akiko, Mae, and I took off running again. I had no idea who she was. But that flip was the best thing I'd ever seen anyone do—that is, anyone who wasn't wearing a cape, mask, and boots!

Twenty-Five

$\mathcal{W}$E TUMBLED BACK INTO ROOM TWELVE, slamming the door shut behind us. It was just beginning to rain, and the afternoon sky had turned gray with clouds. We made sure nobody was trailing us—clowns, monkeys, or otherwise—as we rushed, dripping, into the office. I'd heard Room Twelve had security guards who kept close watch on who came and went. But I had yet to figure out who they were and what they looked like.

"Why so breathless, girls?" asked Mrs. B as we leaned against the door, chests heaving. "Don't tell me you ran up and down San Francisco's hills. This city is quite steep."

"A clown," Mae managed to say. "Aggressive."

Akiko gave her a look. It was clear she wasn't ready to tell Mrs. B about the letter we'd read and her mom possibly helping out the Doll Lady.

"Not Side-Splitter," said Akiko, reassuring Mrs. B. "But still, close enough."

"And menacing," I added, dropping to my knees to scratch Astra's ears. "With friends."

Thunder rattled the windows and rain hammered on the panes. I noticed Mrs. B's expression turn stormy too.

"Side-Splitter might be onto you," she said darkly. "He seems to have an army of clowns just waiting to do his bidding. It's important that you know how to protect yourselves at all times."

Mae began to list off our various superpowers, including the newest ones we'd discovered battling with Side-Splitter. Before Akiko could lodge her complaint about how many we each had, Mrs. B shook her head and said something about homework.

"I've already heard about your run-in. While superpowers are extraordinary gifts reserved for extraordinary times, you must also prepare for what else may come your way. Especially when you least expect it."

Mrs. B crossed to the opposite side of the office, so we followed after her. Opening a heavy door, this one painted a deep blue instead of red like the one leading to Genevieve's code-cracking room, she gestured for us to enter.

Inside was a small gymnasium with pale wooden floors. Barbells lined one wall. A woman seemed to be exercising there, lifting hand weights. When she turned around to face us, I had to blink a few times to believe my eyes.

"You!" I shouted, recognizing the dark-haired woman who'd saved us from the clowns at the waterfront. She had a stronger build than I'd first realized, but her expression was gentle.

"You're the lady who flipped that bad guy!" hollered Akiko. "You're hardly bigger than us!"

"What she means to say," said Mae, though she sounded just as shocked as Akiko and me, "is what a pleasant surprise!"

The woman gave a knowing nod to Mrs. B and set the hand weights on the shelf.

"Mae, Josie, Akiko," came Mrs. B's sharp voice. Whenever she spoke our names, it was like a call to attention. Immediately, the three of us straightened up. "I'd like you to meet a valuable member of our league of secret heroes and a courageous volunteer in our fight against the Nazi evil. This is Noor Khan. She's being briefed for a day or so before shipping out behind enemy lines in France."

We shook hands in an awkward, formal sort of way. I wanted to ask her all sorts of questions, like how she'd flipped that clown and what she was doing at the waterfront. But Akiko plunged ahead the way she always did.

"What does that mean? The bit about *behind enemy lines*?" she asked. "What are you going to be doing?"

"I've been trained to be a radio operator," she explained. "But as you saw earlier today, I'm prepared to fight the enemy in a variety of ways. I was at the waterfront to record observations about a suspicious figure."

Her accent sounded like she came from England, not San Francisco. "In France, I will report on what I see on the ground," she went on. "For example, where the Germans move their troops, how many tanks they have for battle, who in the Resistance needs help with money or weapons. That sort of thing."

I felt my jaw hang open, and I knew my eyes must have been bugging out of their sockets. It sounded like Noor Khan was a spy. Just like my friend Bill back at Gerda's Diner, who used to go by the name Harry Sawyer. I could only imagine the snooping skills she'd been taught! Immediately, I wanted to tell her about ours.

"It's an honor to meet you," said Mae, her good manners on display at all times. "If I may ask, how exactly will you get behind enemy lines? That sounds a little dangerous, doesn't it?"

"I'll parachute in," Agent Khan said, "at night, under the cover of darkness."

"And you're right, Mae. It is dangerous," added Mrs. B. "Noor and the other spies are incredibly brave. They're willing to risk being captured, thrown into prison—even their lives—for our freedoms."

Velvalee Dickinson seemed to be spying, but she wasn't exactly dropping out of the sky from a plane or flipping bad guys over her shoulder. Or at least, I didn't think she was. I wondered what sort of threats lay ahead for Agent Khan. Would they be even worse than what we'd seen with the Hisser and Side-Splitter?

"A-are you ready?" I said, stumbling on my words. "When you face the Nazis in France. Are you ready for them?"

Agent Khan said she'd been through training in Britain. But nothing could ever really prepare a person for the unknown.

"With this in mind," said Mrs. B, "I'd like you three to work with Agent Khan. Akiko, Mae, Josie, you have learned quickly and grown in your individual powers, but—"

"But there's always room to learn more," interrupted a voice from behind us.

We turned to see a figure rise from a high-backed chair at the window. It was Hopscotch! She seemed to fade in and out right before our eyes, like a lightbulb that was about to go out. Smiling patiently, she listened as we bombarded her with questions about where she'd gone, why she'd left, if she could stay longer, and if she'd help us train with Agent Khan.

"Of course I will." Hopscotch laughed. "Now hop to it!"

As Agent Khan kicked her shoes into a corner and Astra curled up on a rug to keep watch, Hopscotch smoothed down her ghostly pale cape and took a deep breath.

"I'd like you to pay close attention to these lessons," Mrs. B said. "We can never have too many tools in the battle—when we're wearing masks and when we're not."

And with a nod to Agent Khan and Hopscotch, Mrs. B slipped into a low chair beside Astra. Like our favorite dog, she seemed to be fighting exhaustion. My heart tensed with worry for them and what seemed to be their waning strength. But as Hopscotch and Agent Khan called us to attention, I had to push those worries away.

"I understand the three of you are very good at solving puzzles and deciphering coded messages," Agent Khan began. "I'd like to show you other kinds of puzzles and how to work them out."

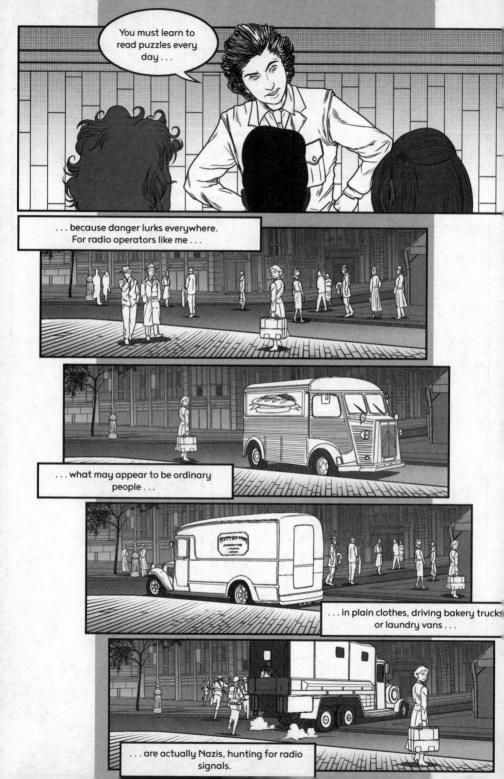

Twenty-Seven

*J*UST AS WE CAUGHT OUR BREATH FROM THE lesson with Hopscotch and Agent Khan, a radio operator rushed into the room waving a note. The cord dangling from her headset trailed behind her like a scarf as she raced over. Mrs. B read the note, and her expression turned grave.

"There's another signal," Mrs. B announced, folding the paper in half and ushering us back into the next room. "Let's hope we can pick up some sort of information about where it's coming from."

Mae, Akiko, and I went right to the corner where we'd worked before and tugged the headsets over our ears. Agent Khan disappeared into the red room.

Again we heard the same call for help: three dots, three dashes, three dots. *S-O-S*.

Static crackled on the line, and I pressed the headset tighter to my ears. I felt as if we were straining with all our might to pick up anything—a voice, a call, even a whisper. I imagined reaching through the airwaves to some secret spot across the ocean and around to the other side of the world.

Listening to the long and short taps of the Morse code, I jotted down what I could. Akiko and Mae did the same in their notebooks. Slowly, bit by bit, we translated the taps into letters and the letters into words. But Mae's pencil flew across her paper faster than mine and Akiko's. She seemed to be able to think and speak in this unusual language echoing over the telegraph lines.

"They're calling for help again," Mae said, her head leaning toward the radio as if that might allow her to hear them more clearly. "It's so faint, I'm afraid I'm missing something."

"Do the best you can," whispered Elizebeth, who had come over to join Mrs. B at our table.

"It's like Hopscotch and Hauntima," whispered Akiko. "A phantom message—there one moment and gone the next."

Akiko was right. These taps were as delicate as cobwebs. I held my breath to hear better, pressing the headset closer to my ears. But moments later, it disappeared.

"What did you two get?" asked Mae as she set her pencil down. "I'm not sure I heard everything."

"Here's what I caught," I said, a little unsure. "'Next ally zone in service.'"

Akiko and Mae turned their notebooks to show they'd written down the same words.

"If they're using the same code as before," whispered Genevieve, who had joined Elizebeth and Mrs. B, "then that spells out N-A-Z-I-S. *Nazis.*"

At the sound of that word, an icy finger sliced down my back.

"The next set," began Akiko, taking a big breath. "It seemed to be: 'Take over whole east region.' T-O-W-E-R."

A look passed between Mrs. B, Elizebeth, and Genevieve.

"*Tower.* What tower do you think they mean?" I asked, searching their faces for an explanation.

But Mrs. B pushed on. "The last line," she urged. "Who thinks they have it?"

Mae volunteered, tapping her pencil on each word she'd deciphered.

"'Put one within easy reach,'" she began. "That spells out P-O-W-E-R. *Power.* And the second part, 'Light end south side,' that's—"

"*Less,*" interrupted Akiko. "What do they mean about less power?"

Mrs. B put her hand down to touch Astra, who was leaning against her leg. "I'm understanding this message to be a warning of Nazi presence, perhaps imprisoning our messenger."

"Towering over them?" asked Mae. "That's a strange word choice."

Elizebeth shook her head. "*Tower* is a place," she said. "I think the messenger is indicating their location."

"They're in a tower somewhere?" asked Akiko, her voice cracking in frustration. "That could be anywhere on earth."

"There's the Tower of London," offered Mae. "That's one of the most famous towers in the world. Maybe they're trapped there, with no electricity."

"The Nazis aren't in London," I said, feeling my throat clench. I could barely get the words out. "They've bombed London, but they haven't *taken over* London."

Genevieve nodded, pushing a pencil behind her ear. I watched as her eyes scanned our notes.

"The last line," she said, running her finger under each word. "The part about power. What could that mean? Are they out of electricity? Weapons? Low on women and men to help?"

"*Power* and *less*," whispered Akiko. "*Powerless.* That's one of the worst feelings in the world."

Mae's breath caught. And at the same moment, I realized the meaning too.

The messenger was desperate. The Nazis had them trapped, and they were *powerless*. I'd felt that way after learning about my father's plane crashing into the Pacific Ocean, taking him from our family forever. Mae felt it every day, worrying about her dad over in France. And Akiko, too, with her family imprisoned in the desert and her brother risking his life in the 442nd Regimental Combat Team.

For each one of us, we knew what it was like to be powerless.

"How do we help?" I asked. "What do we do?"

"When we don't even know where they are," whispered Mae.

"Or what exactly they're up against," added Akiko.

Mrs. B squared her shoulders; then she looked at Akiko, Mae, and me for a few moments. Rain pounded on the windows behind the drawn curtains, thrumming louder with each gust of wind.

"There is only one thing we can do," she said. "Try."

Twenty-Eight

$\mathcal{W}$AIT, THERE'S MORE," CALLED MAE, TUG-ging her headset back over her ears again. "I can hear someone laughing. It's a new voice! Someone has inter-cepted the S-O-S call!"

"That's got to be Side-Splitter again," declared Akiko, pressing a hand to her ear. "I'd know that menacing laugh anywhere. It makes the hair on my arms stand up straight."

I knew it was Side-Splitter too. He had a terrifying laugh that could turn a mug of steaming hot cocoa to ice. The moment he began to speak, I shivered.

"This message is going out to our not-so-super friend overseas." He was cackling. "Boo-hoo! You're sad and lonely. Listen up," he snarled, his menacing laugh turning into a growl. "Side-Splitter's army is coming for you!"

"He doesn't even bother to put anything in code," marveled Mae. "I guess he figures nobody can stop him!"

"I hope he's wrong about that," whispered Mrs. B.

Static crackled again on the line, but Side-Splitter's menacing voice cut through the noise. "We have eyes and ears everywhere. We'll sink every battleship, every aircraft carrier, and every destroyer on the sea! We'll stop at nothing, even when it's raining gnats and frogs."

Akiko froze.

I couldn't even hear her breathe.

She stared into Mrs. B's face as her own turned ashen.

The radio signal faded, and Side-Splitter's hideous laugh thankfully disappeared into the static and hum.

Mrs. B leaned closer to Elizebeth and Genevieve, the three of them launching into discussion about what to make of the crazed clown's threats. Mae pulled her headset down and let it hang around her neck. I scooted my chair closer to the two of them.

"It's her," Akiko whispered. Her hands gripped her pencil. "My mom is working with them. I was hoping she was innocent, that she was somehow oblivious to what the Doll Lady was doing. Maybe just helping repair the dolls or something. But did you hear what Side-Splitter said? The words he used?"

Mae leaned forward, whispering so that Mrs. B and the others wouldn't hear. "The Doll Lady must have reported to Side-Splitter. Because he mentioned the exact three ships from the letter—the ones she was watching at the waterfront."

"I'm guessing her letters go to the Japanese military," I suggested. "And she also—"

"No," Akiko interrupted, closing her eyes tight. "Didn't you hear that phrase? The one Side-Splitter said at the end?"

My mind raced, replaying his words. The battleship. The superheroes in danger. Eyes and ears everywhere.

"What is it?" asked Mae gently, reaching her hand across the table to squeeze Akiko's. "Tell us what you heard."

"That phrase," Akiko said hoarsely. "It's a giveaway. Everyone knows it's *raining cats and dogs*. But not my mom. She always mixes that expression up and says *raining gnats and frogs*. She was animal crazy my whole life. She couldn't stand the idea of cats and dogs being stuck outside in the rain. So that phrase—that's how I know it's her.

"My mom is working for Side-Splitter too!"

I shook my head, trying to rattle some sense back into it. Because suddenly things were starting to feel like too much.

"Akiko, that can't be right," I said, keeping my voice low. "Your brother is in the army. Didn't you say he signed up with other boys, right there in the internment camp? There's no way—"

"I can't explain it," Akiko said, her voice full of emotion. She wasn't the crying type, but I still looked away.

"It doesn't make sense right now, Akiko," whispered Mae. "But we don't have to believe it. There must be some explanation we're not thinking of. There has to be some logical reason for this . . ."

"It's her." Akiko's voice was rough and low, and I had to lean in to hear her. "I can't explain it, but she's involved with Side-Splitter."

"You're wrong. I just know it, Akiko. How could she possibly line up with him?" I said, unable to speak his terrible name. "He's pure evil! He's willing to hurt innocent people, the way the Nazis are doing in Europe! It doesn't make any sense."

Akiko looked away. I imagined how awful I would feel if I believed Mam or my brothers or anyone in my family was misleading me.

"There has to be more to the story," Mae said. She always tried to look on the sunny side of things. But as thunder rattled in the distance and rain started up another noisy patter on the windowpanes, that was becoming harder to do.

Twenty-Nine

$\mathcal{B}$EFORE LONG, GENEVIEVE AND ELIZEBETH returned to their desks and their notebooks and their radio headsets. They were on the front line of intercepting messages like Side-Splitter's and the coded secrets meant for the Japanese military. And Mrs. B returned to us.

"It's time we look for our not-so-funny friend Side-Splitter," she said, tying the belt of her raincoat with a firm tug. Astra stretched his legs beside her. "And while we're at it, we should look for the Doll Lady as well."

Akiko jumped to her feet.

"That's okay, Mrs. B! We can do it," she said. "Don't worry about a thing. You stay here and—"

"I'm glad we'll go together," Mae said, giving Akiko a firm look. "Maybe you can help us make sense of what's happening."

Akiko's jaw dropped, and I heard her take a few deep breaths before following the rest of us out the door into the rain. It was falling in a steady downpour, and the three of us walked together behind Mrs. B, who was sheltering Astra beneath her umbrella. I was grateful Akiko had popped open her own. And that it was big enough to cover both Mae and me too.

When the rain stopped minutes later, I still wanted to stay close together underneath Akiko's umbrella. I felt safe there. But she shook off the water and folded it up, tucking it back into her bag. Mrs. B closed up hers and began to use it like a cane, probably for help with her bad leg.

She seemed to know where she wanted to go, so we walked in silence behind her and Astra, up steep hills and down twisting sidewalks. But our pace wasn't what I'd call brisk or anything.

"Astra, do you need a rest?" asked Mae, leaning down at a corner stoplight near a bakery and scratching Astra's fluffy ears. "Or maybe a bowl of water?"

Mrs. B seemed as if she could use a break too. But she never complained.

Astra sat down on the sidewalk, looking tired. Cars and delivery vans passed us in all directions. It wasn't the best place to take a break, but I wasn't going to push him. His tongue lolled out the side of his mouth, and he panted to catch his breath. As he lowered his front legs to lie down for a full nap, Mrs. B leaned back against the side of the bakery's wooden building. She seemed as tired as Astra.

"You're observant girls," Mrs. B began. "I know Astra and I can't fool you."

Mae sat down on the sidewalk beside Astra and scratched her knuckles over his eyebrows. His eyes closed as he wagged his tail.

"Our strength is slipping. Day by day, Astra has been slowing down. As have I."

"Mrs. B, that happens to everyone, doesn't it?" I asked. "My mother says it comes with getting—"

"Old?" she said. "We don't grow old. We just grow more experienced. But this slowing down isn't normal. This is different. My legs move as if weights were hanging around my ankles. My arms are spaghetti."

Akiko studied Mrs. B's face like she was looking at a painting in an art museum.

"You're not wrinkly or anything," she declared. Mae poked Akiko with her shoe to be quiet, but Akiko ignored her. "I'm not being rude, Mae. Mrs. B isn't an old lady. She's still young."

"Astra is too," Mrs. B said, her eyes sad as she watched him rest his head on Mae's lap. "Something is doing this to us. And I fear it's the same force that's sapping the energy of our superheroes."

"No!" I shouted, though I didn't mean to be so loud. "That can't happen! We need you, Mrs. B! It's bad enough that Hauntima was just a ghost of herself. And that Hopscotch is practically transparent. But you? We can't lose you, too, Mrs. B!"

Mrs. B pushed away from the building and signaled for Astra to join her. Then she set off climbing the steep sidewalk ahead of us, into the rush of San Francisco's afternoon.

"I don't plan on disappearing anytime soon," she said, her words drifting back to us over her shoulder. "But even if I did, you girls have proven yourselves worthy. You've stood side by side with the ENIAC Six. You've demonstrated great skill with the best code crackers of the war. And you've learned to sharpen your talents with one of the most daring spies of our time. I see only great things ahead."

I couldn't stop the flutter that rose in my chest. Sure, we'd had a few good moments as superheroes. But Zenobia had been the most powerful superhero the world had ever known, and now she was missing. If Mrs. B and Astra disappeared too, what would happen to us?

"We'll keep on trying," Mae said. "But, Mrs. B, please let us help you and Astra."

"Mae's right," Akiko said. "You've got to let us know how to stop this force that's draining you. Before it's too late. You mean too much to us. Not only you," she said. And surprisingly, Akiko reached a hand out to scratch Astra's brown-and-white fur beside her. "Astra means the world to us too."

Thirty

WE CROSSED A BUSY STREET, AND I SAW people ahead of us lined up to ride the cable cars over a nearby hill. The clatter of their bells cut through the noisy crowds and passing trucks. I noticed Mae had a funny expression on her face.

"What are you grinning about?" I asked.

"Oh, nothing," Mae said. But her eyes seemed to indicate otherwise. She reached down and gave Astra's head an affectionate rub.

"Really," urged Akiko, "what is it?"

"Well, the way you were so nice to Astra just now," Mae said. "I knew you loved dogs. You can't fool me."

I laughed, and Mrs. B joined in too. But Akiko's face turned serious.

"It's easier that way," she said. And I caught a sadness in her voice that I'd never heard before.

"Easier?" I said. "What do you mean, Akiko?"

She shrugged and looked away.

"I'm so sorry, Akiko," Mae said. "I didn't mean to stir up—"

"Acting like I don't care is easier than talking about it," she began, turning back to us. "When we heard about the president's order—I told you, Executive Order 9066, the one that sent all the Japanese families like mine to the camps—my parents didn't want us to worry. They tried not to let us know what they were going through—all the anxiety they were feeling about losing Dad's business, having to sell our home and things, all of it."

I nodded. I understood, but in so many ways, I knew I never really could.

"One day, we came home, and our dogs were missing," Akiko went on. "Daisy and Moose—those were their names. My brother, Tommy, and I looked for them for hours, calling for them up and down the streets in the whole neighborhood. They'd never gone missing before."

She paused, and I could see her cheeks flush pink. Mae reached over and put a hand on Akiko's shoulder.

"The next morning, my parents said everything was

okay. That Daisy and Moose were happy. They told us they'd given them to friends who lived in another part of the city, outside of Japantown."

"That's great," I said softly. "So Daisy and Moose weren't lost after all."

Akiko shook her head.

"That's what my parents wanted us to believe." Her voice was tight, and I knew she was having a hard time getting the words out. "Later I found out from my uncle that somebody had poisoned them."

Mae shot a hand to her mouth. I stumbled on a crack in the sidewalk, nearly falling down. Suddenly, the realization hit me like a splash of cold water:

Akiko didn't hate dogs. She loved them. She loved them so much, it hurt—so much that she could hardly touch them for the memories they stirred up about her own dogs. Mam hadn't let us get a dog, but I still loved animals—from hummingbirds all the way to elephants and giraffes. Just thinking about someone doing harm to an innocent, trusting creature made me want to throw my arms around Astra's neck and hug him tight. How could anyone harm an animal?

But first I reached out and hugged Akiko.

It must have been so hard for her all this time. It was as if she'd been wearing a mask—putting up a stern face to pretend that she didn't care, when underneath, she was devastated.

We walked on until we got to the line for the cable cars and stood waiting with all the other people. I knew Akiko wouldn't like any of us making a fuss over her. Mrs. B seemed to understand too. Her eyes were full of sadness as she reached over and took Akiko's hand in her own, quietly letting her know that she understood. Astra leaned against Akiko's leg. Mae wiped at her eyes.

There were so many things I wanted to say or even shout. But instead I just stayed put next to Akiko, trying to tell her everything by simply standing beside her.

"When we talk about the Infinity Trinity's work," Akiko whispered, her eyes lingering on Astra's wiry coat, "I think of Daisy and Moose along with everybody else.

"If we don't stand up for them, who will?"

Thirty-One

$\mathcal{A}$NOTHER STREET ENTERTAINER WAS BUSY at work not far from us. The high-pitched strumming of a ukulele caught our attention. And as we waited for the cable car to return down the steep hill and for the gripmen to spin it around, we fixed our focus on the music. The song was about some gal in Kalamazoo.

"Is that another clown?" I asked, nodding toward the tall, skinny ukulele player. I was suspicious of everyone now. "This whole city seems to be filled with them."

"I bet it is," answered Mae. "I don't see the same hat Side-Splitter wore, but maybe they still do his bidding." Then she nudged my shoulder and gestured toward another, this one short and squat and doing card tricks for tourists. "And look! They seem to know each other."

As we stood quietly in line, it was easy to listen in on the conversations around us. Two men behind us were talking about going fishing. The couple ahead of us was deciding what restaurant they wanted to try this evening. And now the chatter between the two performers carried on the breeze over to our ears.

"Hey, you new in town?" asked the tall one, still playing the ukulele. "Haven't seen you before."

"Sure am," said the short one. And then he glanced furtively in either direction before stepping closer to his tall acquaintance. "Hey," he asked in a serious tone, "why did the clown go to the doctor?"

The tall one froze, his fingers stopping midstrum.

"Because," he answered, his words coming out stiff and precise, "he felt a little funny."

They stared at each other for just a beat, neither one laughing at the corny joke. Then they grabbed their things and began moving along together. I assumed they were heading off to some other spot, where they could put out a hat and collect coins from passersby. As they walked away, I saw the tall performer slip a note to the smaller one. I wondered what it said.

"Here it is," Mrs. B announced as the cable car clanged its bell, signaling for us to climb aboard. "Let's go!"

Mae and Akiko tucked onto a bench with Mrs. B and Astra. I took hold of a strap that dangled from the car's ceiling and stood beside them. While Astra closed his eyes, I knew Mrs. B was looking out for Side-Splitter.

"He could be anywhere in the city," she said, her voice loud enough for only the three of us to hear. "I say *he*. But really we must think in terms of a possible army of Side-Splitters. He has bands of evildoers who seem willing to carry out his dastardly deeds."

Another army of evil clowns? This was the sort of stuff that could give a kid nightmares! I peeked over at Mae, and I saw that her eyes were wide. Akiko looked just as watchful.

She reached into her Hauntima bag and pulled out socks and her black-and-white saddle shoes. As she slipped them on and tucked her sandals away, Akiko mumbled something about the best footwear for fighting villains.

The cable car strained its way up the hill, climbing higher and higher toward what felt like the clouds. The views of the city suddenly became magnificent as we crested the peak, and the silvery blue bay stretched out in the distance. The heavy clouds had thankfully burned off, and the streets seemed bathed in a golden light.

As we made a stop to pick up more passengers, I couldn't help but notice another street performer climb on with the rest of the new riders. She tucked a harmonica in her pocket as she grabbed a strap beside Mrs. B and hung on.

Mae jabbed an elbow into my rib cage, letting me know she'd spied her too. "At least it's not another clown," she whispered. I let out a sigh of relief.

The bell clanged noisily, and we set off again. The wind whipped our hair, and my stomach surged into my throat as we sped downhill. Plunging down San Francisco's hills in a cable car was a pretty good way to get around, at least when flying and teleporting weren't options.

"Let's get off here and see what's what," Mrs. B said as we reached a stop on a busy cross-street.

I jumped off and looked all around at the tall buildings and crowded sidewalks. Mae and Akiko did the same, their heads tilted back and their eyes taking in everything as they turned in circles.

"Excuse me," said the harmonica lady from the cable car. She had walked up to someone who was bent over and tying his shoe. Only it wasn't an ordinary shoe; it was oversize and red with long black laces. My breath caught, and I wheezed as if someone had slugged me in the stomach.

There was only one type of person who would wear a shoe like that. A clown.

"I was wondering," the harmonica lady went on, her voice quiet. "Why did the clown go to the doctor?"

Slowly the man with the oversize shoes stood up. He

nodded to the harmonica lady and gave his answer, low and secretive. "Because he was feeling funny."

Mae froze.

Akiko coughed.

"Look," I whispered. I started to point, but Mae swatted my arm. "Harmonica Lady is passing him a note!"

"We've got to find out what that message says," Mae said. "Let's follow them!"

We signaled to Mrs. B and Astra to cross the street, and we made our way down the block behind the suspicious pair. Mrs. B seemed to catch on immediately, and she and Astra dodged a passing truck and fell in behind us. Astra still looked weak, but he kept up.

"These clowns," I began, "they're all telling each other the same joke."

"What does it mean?" asked Mae, her eyes never leaving the dangerous duo up ahead of us.

"It means they're not very original," said Akiko. "Why tell the same corny joke over and over?"

Mrs. B stared ahead of us up the street. Another clown was performing, this time on stilts. He towered over the crowd as children ran back and forth and vendors sold popcorn and balloons. It seemed to be a street carnival.

"That's a good question, Akiko," she said. Astra let out a heavy sigh as he sat down on the sidewalk beside her and rested. "These particular clowns are not in the business of being amusing. They're as dangerous as knives."

We pressed in closer together as we studied the scene up ahead.

"I suspect it's no coincidence that we're seeing so many of them around the city today," Mrs. B said. "And that joke you've been hearing could be their own particular signal."

"Signal?" said Mae. "For what?"

I didn't wait for Mrs. B to respond. The very thought of these clowns teaming up together to do Side-Splitter's bidding sent a tremor of fear through my whole body like a little earthquake.

"For carrying out their evil plan," I said. "Let's go!"

Thirty-Two

WE RUSHED DEEPER INTO THE STREET CAR-
nival. Music played from a small bandshell in the adjoining
park, and swing dancers spun and twirled in a colorful
whirl of action. A handful of men and women gathered
nearby and chatted as kids raced past us on tricycles.
Pigeons trailed after them, probably hoping to gobble up
fallen crackers and popcorn.

"Watch the performer on stilts," whispered Mrs. B.
"Let's see if we can intercept a note."

We studied his antics for a few moments. He tipped his
hat to the harmonica lady, who by now had pulled out a
bowler hat and put it on. Together with her friend in the

oversize shoes, they disappeared deeper into the crowd.

"We've got to get that message," agreed Mae. "But how? I don't want to knock him down from his stilts. That seems a little violent. And what if he's innocent? What if it's just a note about a new circus in town?"

Mrs. B agreed with Mae's caution.

"Then we'll just ask him," Akiko announced. And reaching into her Hauntima bag, she pulled out her umbrella. She popped it open, then began pretending she was in a high-wire act at the circus. Tilting the umbrella from side to side, she pantomimed crossing a tightrope.

"You have everything we'll ever need in that bag." Mae laughed.

"I'm a Girl Scout," Akiko said with a shrug. "We're always prepared. Now clear out so he doesn't get suspicious."

Mrs. B and Astra headed for a bench under a eucalyptus tree. Mae and I skirted the edge of the dance area, keeping our eyes on the entertainer. He was easy enough to track, since his stilts made him a good three or four feet taller than everyone else.

Akiko slinked closer, twirling her umbrella and acting like a tightrope walker.

"I'm new in town," I heard her say, her face turned up to the towering performer. "I wonder, do you know why the clown went to the doctor?"

And just as we knew he'd respond, the man on stilts

lowered his head and said, "Because he was feeling funny." But then he paused and sized up Akiko with a suspicious stare. "Good golly, the recruits are getting younger and younger. Are you really one of us?"

Akiko nodded but kept up the pantomime. I knew her voice must have been stuck in her throat. Finally, she managed to speak, though what came out of her mouth sounded like gears grinding. "I'm older—*ahem*—than I appear."

That seemed to satisfy him. He reached into the pocket of his long, baggy pants and pulled out a note. Folding it tight, he looked all around as if making sure nobody was witnessing the exchange. When his eyes landed on Mae and me in the crowd, suddenly Mae stomped on my foot.

"Ouch!" I shouted. "What'd you do that for?"

Mae grabbed my arm and turned me away. "So he wouldn't think we were watching him," she whispered, her breath hot in my hair. "Keep walking!"

I caught sight of Mrs. B and Astra getting to their feet across the park. Glancing over my shoulder, I could see Akiko walking briskly up the sidewalk behind us.

When we were a block or so away from the carnival, Mae pointed toward a library. So we ducked inside and over to a long wooden table near a stained glass window. Mrs. B arrived moments later, and Astra lay down at her feet under the table. He panted to catch his breath. Mae whispered something about Granny Crumpler never allowing dogs into her library, but I was grateful Astra was so quiet and hadn't drawn the attention of any of the busy librarians.

Not even a minute passed before Akiko burst through the library door. She could still be noisy without speaking a word, pushing past chairs and catching her breath as she made her way over to us. But instead of finding it annoying, I found it endearing. Our wheezy, asthmatic, mouth breather had been incredibly brave.

She plunked down into a chair and slapped the note on the table.

"I think it's the real deal," she announced in her best whisper. "Look!"

Before we could begin reading, a couple behind us scooted their chairs away from their table and stood up. Mrs. B tilted her head, and I could tell she was listening to their conversation. So I listened too. Mae and Akiko went silent beside me.

"A circus?" the man was saying as he picked up a bulky book. "Where is it?"

"On the waterfront," whispered the woman, adjusting her own stack of books. "My mom says there's elephants and clowns and everything!"

"Hey, I heard a good joke the other day," the man went on. "Why don't cannibals eat clowns?"

Thirty-Three

"BECAUSE THEY—" BEGAN MAE, JUMPING right into their conversation.

"Taste—" interrupted Akiko. But she just stared at the couple, leaving the joke unfinished.

"Funny," I said. Though I found nothing at all funny about his joke.

Mae, Akiko, and I sprang to our feet, as if the book-toting man had lit a stick of dynamite. Was he another maniacal clown? Did he know who we were? Was he sending a signal to clowns around us to launch a full attack? In a library?

"Hey, you've heard that one before," he said, turning to us with a broad smile. "I thought it was a real knee-slapper.

What about the one where the chicken crossed—"

Suddenly a librarian appeared looking deeply annoyed. She shushed the couple and hurried them toward the front desk, asking them to show their library cards.

"What was that all about?" whispered Mae with a gasp. "Is he a clown too?"

"I don't think so," I said, looking over my shoulder as they checked out their books. "I think he was just a guy who tells bad jokes."

"Sometimes it's hard to spot the difference," Mrs. B began, "between an innocent coincidence and a well-planned scheme. As you know, we look for patterns. What we detected earlier today was the same joke passed from one clown to another. This gentleman's joke, I believe, was a not-so-funny coincidence."

"Did you hear that, Akiko?" asked Mae. "About coincidences? They happen all the time. But they can be explained away."

I knew Mae was thinking about Akiko's mom and how she might not really be working to help the Doll Lady. Mae still believed it was a coincidence. But Akiko didn't look convinced.

Akiko turned back to the note, unfolding it at the table. The rest of us slid our chairs closer together—both to better see what was written on the page, but also to keep from stirring up the sharp-eared librarian.

On the paper were a bunch of numbers written in pencil. It was laid out in a grid format, but the only pattern I could see seemed to be at the bottom, where there were a bunch of number fives.

"If only we'd brought Genevieve with us," I whispered. "She'd probably know exactly how to read this message."

"Or Elizebeth," said Mae. "Seems like she's always up for a challenge."

"Elizebeth is busy trying to solve the Doll Lady case," Mrs. B said. "And catch any of Velvalee Dickinson's accomplices."

Akiko's face fell.

"The three of you have more talent than you give yourselves credit for," Mrs. B went on. "Believe in your own power."

"And try," whispered Mae, sitting up a little straighter in her chair.

"Yes." Mrs. B smiled. "Just try. It's only a matter of taking that first step."

Akiko squared her shoulders, like she was ready for a fight, and I scooted my chair in a little closer. As I gazed down at the page again, I could hear voices in my head. *Stitch by stitch*, Kay had taught me. *Look for the patterns*, Genevieve had reminded us. *Open your mind*, Agent Khan had said.

We stared at the writing. There were four lines of numbers, some repeating, but not all of them.

52 15 11 41 35 34

24 44

13 11 12 32 15

13 11 43

"At the bottom there," said Mae, tapping the paper. "What do you think that means? It's a bit of a pattern."

Those two notes penciled at the bottom had caught my attention too. They read:

5X5

505

"Xs and Os mean love," suggested Akiko. "Is this about five people in love?"

"Is 505 a type of ship?" asked Mae. "Maybe it's got something to do with the navy and another battleship or destroyer."

"We already know a lot about the navy," I said. "And the ships Side-Splitter has his eye on."

Mrs. B nodded, then peeked under the table to check on Astra. He let out a deep sigh and laid his head on her feet. A moment later, he was asleep. I felt a surge of worry shoot straight to my heart. Poor Astra! He seemed to be getting weaker by the day. We had to solve this message fast and stop whatever deadly plan Side-Splitter was plotting! If we didn't, who knew what would happen to Astra and Mrs. B? And to Zenobia, as well as all kinds of innocent people here in San Francisco and even around the world!

Akiko must have been feeling the same frantic worry. Because she plunged her hand into her canvas bag and felt around until she found pencils and a notebook.

"Here, for each of us," she said, tearing pages out and passing them around the table. "Surely we can solve this thing if we just give it a try."

Mae's pencil scratched across her page. Akiko tapped the eraser at her temple, as if poking her brain into action. I stared at the beautiful tile ceiling above us, trying to calm my mind and focus.

"If A is the number one, B is the number two," I heard Akiko whispering to herself. Mae's mumblings were quieter, and I could only catch a "let's see" and "hmph" now and then.

I let my eyes linger over the numbers on the page again, running through all the possibilities I could think of. But I kept circling back to the line near the bottom: *5X5.*

"That's it!" I shouted. A librarian passing the shelves behind us let out a long "*Sssshhhhhhhhh.*" I lowered my voice before going on, and we all leaned in even closer together.

"Where it reads five X five, that has to mean 'five by five.' Elizebeth mentioned it yesterday when we were at her desk. I bet this message is written in the form of five letters across and five letters up and down."

"You're probably right, Josie!" said Akiko. "These clowns aren't too bright. So it's likely they wrote that hint—five by five—right there on the page to help their clown friends solve the cipher!"

"And look," exclaimed Mae, whose pencil never stopped moving. "I think I'm already cracking it."

Thirty-Four

$\mathcal{M}$AE SLID HER PAPER TO THE CENTER OF the table, where she'd whipped out a quick grid, five columns across and five rows down. "Five multiplied by five equals twenty-five. Since there are twenty-six letters in the alphabet and not twenty-five, I bet they doubled up on two letters."

"Probably the letters we use the least—like *U* and *V*," suggested Akiko.

I studied the message's grid and copied it onto my own paper, to double-check.

	1	2	3	4	5
1	A	B	C	D	E
2	F	G	H	I	J
3	K	L	M	N	O
4	P	Q	R	S	T
5	UV	W	X	Y	Z

"It looks good," I whispered, glancing around to make sure no joke-telling readers, quiet-loving librarians, or even creepy clowns were around to hear us. "What do we think they're saying?"

"Let's start with the shortest line," Mae said, copying it down onto her paper again as we all watched.

24 44

"First numbers, two and four. If we go over to column two," she went on, pencil scratching, "and down to row four—"

"That lands on a *Q*," Akiko interrupted. "And over four, down four gives us an *S*. Q-S doesn't spell anything."

"Right," I said. "Let's try going down two rows first, then over four columns. When we do that, we get—"

"Down two, over four is *I*," croaked Akiko. "And down four, over four is still *S*. And I-S spells *IS*! That *is* something!"

Our eyes danced as we looked at each other and Mrs. B. We were going to crack this clown message, there was no doubting that!

"The next two lines have repeated numbers," I said, running my pencil beneath them. "That will make it easier to solve."

I wrote down:

13 11 12 32 15
13 11 43

"Down one, over three," said Mae, her words coming fast in her excitement. "Those are both *C*s. And down one, over one—those are both *A*s, of course."

I wrote down:

C A _ _ _
C A _

"One down, over two is *B*," Akiko said in her breathless whisper. "That's so easy."

"And down four, over three is . . . ," I added, pencil racing up and down, "an *R*. The second word is C-A-R! *Car!*"

We had:

C A B _ _
C A R

"Cab car!" said Akiko. "What is that? Like a taxi?"

Mae solved the last two letters: *L* and *E*.

"It's not a taxi," she said, nudging Akiko with her shoulder. "It's the best way to get around San Francisco! *Cable car!*"

"I wonder what it's saying," I said, my voice like a mouse's squeak as a few patrons passed our table. "Maybe this is a clue about *where* the clowns are supposed to meet. Do you think the location could be painted on the side of a cable car? Or *when* they're supposed to meet? Or maybe one of the clowns is driving a cable car—now, that's a scary idea."

Mae's head was down as she scribbled on her paper, working out the top line of the puzzle. When she looked up, her eyes were unfocused, as if she were dizzy. Mrs. B reached over and patted Mae's hand.

"What, Mae?" she urged. "Tell us."

"It's not a place or a time," she whispered. "That top line spells W-E-A-P-O-N. This message means . . ." She paused, unable to speak the words she'd just deciphered.

"Side-Splitter's weapon," I said, barely able to make sense of the words I was reading, "is going to be a cable car."

Akiko pushed her chair away. "How much time do you think we have?"

I jumped to my feet, pointing toward the front door of the library.

"Judging by all those clowns we've already seen today," I said, my voice rising to a panicky yell, "I—I think it's happening right now!"

Thirty-Five

$\mathcal{E}$CHOES OF "*SHHHHHHHH*" AND "*QUIET!*" trailed behind us as we rushed through the library doors and out into the crowded flow of people on the sidewalk. Since the rain had cleared and the weather was sunny and beautiful again, the whole city seemed to have come outside to enjoy it.

"We have to get to the cable-car line," shouted Akiko, "right away!"

"Think of all the innocent people who could be hurt by Side-Splitter and those clowns," whispered Mae, her eyes panning the crowds around us. "We've got to stop this madness."

I wanted to transform into the Infinity Trinity and soar into the air as fast as we could. But something was holding me back.

"Mrs. B," I said, turning to her and Astra. "If only you could come with us. I wish you still had the strength."

"We could use your quick thinking," Mae said.

"And the power of the Palomino, Star, and their moonstones," added Akiko.

She shook her head. "I will be with you in spirit," she said. "Know that, girls, please. If Astra and I could, we'd be flying right beside you."

Her voice was steady, but her eyes revealed her sadness. I noticed something else there too. Anger. Frustration at whatever was sapping their strength. Standing before her and Astra and seeing how powerless they'd become, well, I felt angry too.

"We'll do all we can to fight this," I said. "Not just for Zenobia, but for you, too."

"Astra and I will make our way there. But now is the time for you to act. Try your hardest."

We dashed down an alleyway beside the library and grabbed each other's shoulders. Now, more than ever, the words we spoke rang in my ears. As streams of purple, orange, and green swirled before my eyes, I realized our purpose wasn't about danger or adventure or any silly motto. When we transformed into the Infinity Trinity, we really were about protecting innocents from harm, fighting for justice, and doing whatever good we possibly could.

"Onward and upward!" hollered Mae. And we soared above the library, scanning the streets below us for any sign of Side-Splitter.

"The cable cars are this way!" shouted Akiko over the noisy wind and our flapping capes. "We just need to fly above this hill and around Coit Tower."

I wasn't sure what Coit Tower was, but when I saw a tall monument that looked like a fire hose pointing toward the stars, I figured this was it. I kept my eyes busy, searching below us for the cable-car lines and any funny business. Funny as in crazed clowns.

"Hauntima's ghost!" shouted Mae. "Look—"

"Hey, that's my line," interrupted Akiko.

"What's the big deal, Violet?" I asked. "Is it Side-Splitter? A clown car full of dangerous criminals?"

Without answering, Mae circled the sky in a few low loops. Finally, she landed on the top of the tower. Akiko and I followed.

"I said we'd fly *over* Coit Tower," Akiko croaked, "not land on it."

"Don't you see what's down there?" asked Mae, catching her breath. "A pink pancake! I think it's the Doll Lady. And your mom!"

The three of us rushed to the edge of the tower and

looked down on the street below. Though I noticed Mae stepped back from the edge, keeping her eyes looking up rather than down at the ground so far below us. She really did seem to be afraid of heights.

"How can you be sure it's them?" I said, taking in all I could see, up and down the street. I couldn't find the pancake hat. Or the green beret.

"We need binoculars," muttered Akiko as she felt around in the pouch at her waist. "Surely there's something in here." And she whipped out what at first looked like her round sunglasses. But when she held them to her eyes, they became fancy binoculars.

"Yes!" I said, eager to try them out. "Let's see!"

"It's so clear now," she said, "as if these things give me super-vision. I can see one, two, three, four people. They're talking. Two of them are women. They're wearing . . ."

I heard her breath catch.

"That's definitely Velvalee Dickinson," she said, her voice so low, I had to step closer to hear her. Mae did too. "And that's my mom with her. They're handing something to those two clowns. It looks like a toy or . . ."

Akiko pulled the binoculars away and shoved them into my hands. She looked stricken as she turned her back on the view. Instead she stared up into the sky.

"Okay, I see them," I said, adjusting my eyes to the binoculars and focusing in on the foursome below. "They're holding—wait, it's not a toy." My vision was crisp and clear. Almost too clear, as what I saw made my stomach hurt. "Your mom. She's holding one thing while Velvalee is turning the other thing around in her hands. I think it's . . . it's . . ."

I couldn't get the words out.

Mae took the binoculars. Then she gasped.

"It can't be. It's really . . ."

Mae lowered the binoculars and stared at me, her jaw slack and her eyes sad.

"Say it," Akiko croaked, whipping around to face us again. "Say it!"

Mae lifted the binoculars back to her eyes.

"It's a ring," Mae whispered. "I can see the stone in the center—it's white. And Velvalee is holding a dog's collar. It has the same white jewel. They . . . they look familiar. Like—"

"Moonstones." Akiko's cheeks were flushed. "There's only one animal who wears a moonstone collar. And that is Star, sidekick to the Palomino."

Mae lowered the binoculars. And now she turned her back on the view too.

"I think this must have something to do with why Astra and Mrs. B have become so weak," she said, trying desperately to make sense of what was happening. "In taking away part of their superhero costume, somehow it's taking away their powers, too."

The Doll Lady had Mrs. B's moonstone ring? And Astra's moonstone collar? Panic whirled inside me like a milkshake in a blender. What would happen if Side-Splitter got ahold of them? Would he gain the superpowers that belonged to the Palomino and Star?

"We've got to get those moonstones back," I said, "before it's too late for Mrs. B and Astra!"

"And we've got to reach the cable cars before anyone gets hurt," Mae said. "Not to mention stop Side-Splitter, his clown army, the Doll Lady—"

"And my mom," whispered Akiko, shoving the binoculars back into the pouch at her waist. "There's so much that needs to be done. Let's go."

Thirty-Six

$\mathcal{S}$HOULD I CREATE A STORM AND BLOW THE
moonstones out of the Doll Lady's hands?" called Mae as
we circled high above the foursome on the street. My eyes
never left the pink pancake below us.

"Or maybe I should shape-shift into a claw and snatch
them," Akiko offered. "But who knows what these clowns
are capable of. What if Side-Splitter gave them powers?"

Mrs. B's voice echoed in my mind like a drumbeat: *Try.
Take the leap. Do something.* When things get hard, we can't
give up or shrug our shoulders or look to someone else. The
only thing we can do is *try.*

"This will require all three of us," I said, hovering

beside them. "I'll use my telekinesis to pull the moonstones to me. But I'll need you both to distract the clowns."

Akiko and Mae knew just what to do. They dipped lower, over the rooftops across the street from the foursome. Velvalee was just reaching out her hands to pass the dog collar to one of the clowns when Mae spun a small tornado. It whipped down from the sky and stirred up the trees and bushes all along the street as it raced toward the four figures. Akiko's mom and the Doll Lady shot their hands to their heads to keep their hats from blowing away. The clowns covered their eyes from the dust.

Akiko flicked her fingers, and sparks shot from the top of the tornado like candles on a dangerous birthday cake. It was a showy display of their skills, and I felt a rush of pride for the Infinity Trinity. But it also made me a little self-conscious. What if I didn't measure up?

There was no time to hesitate. The clowns began shouting, which caused the Doll Lady and Akiko's mom to pull back. So I zeroed in on the moonstones, and with all my might, I imagined them tracing an arc through the air and into my hands.

"Come to me," I whispered, focusing my powers of telekinesis. "Now!"

And like two shooting stars, the ring and the dog collar soared through the sky from their fingertips to mine. The milky white moonstones glimmered with life.

"Got 'em!"

Mae and Akiko were beside me in a flash, and I slipped the collar and ring into Akiko's gadget bag for safekeeping.

"Let's round up these meanies so the police can take care of them," Mae said, sounding a little like my brother Baby Lou. "We don't want the Doll Lady getting away. Or those evil clowns!"

But as we started to circle back, I heard a strange whipping sound in the air above us. Could it be capes? Were more superheroes arriving to help us? Or was it the beat of wings and Mae's helpful birds flying to the rescue?

When I turned my eyes skyward, I caught sight of an enormous red kite. And beside it, three or four more of them were soaring over the city, their long tails snapping behind them. And as if in slow motion, the biggest of the kites suddenly burst into flames. A thundering explosion followed, along with a high-pitched laugh that was all too familiar. I had to adjust my mask to make sure I wasn't seeing things as the burning kite took the shape of a terrible clown face. His ball-like nose, wild hair, and laughing mouth were clearly defined.

"That's Side-Splitter!" shouted Mae. The blood rushed from my arms, and I felt as if I would drop from the sky like a stone.

"The time has come for serious clowning around!" boomed his voice. It seemed to echo off Coit Tower, the nearby buildings, and the treetops—even throughout the whole city. "Let's have a little fun! Shall we?"

An eerie cheer erupted in response, echoing loudest from the waterfront. Side-Splitter's clowns must have already been waiting for him there.

"The bridges!" Akiko shouted. "And the ships—he wants to destroy them!"

"And the cable car," I called as we began soaring toward the bay. "He's going to use one as a weapon!"

"Let's get closer," Mae said in her steady voice. "If we can put Side-Splitter in our sights, I can use my mental telepathy and find out what's going through that twisted mind of his!"

Side-Splitter's terrifying laugh pulsed through the air like a shock wave, making the landscape beneath us shudder. I shivered at the sound of it despite the warmth of the afternoon sun. Because of all the places in the world we could possibly go right now, Side-Splitter's mind seemed like the scariest of all.

Thirty-Eight

"SOMEBODY HELP!" CAME A SHOUT BEHIND us. "This dog's not gonna make it!"

Mae and Akiko were helping Hopscotch's grainy form to her feet. I whipped around and saw a crowd gathering around the cable car where it had come off its tracks. I knew right away what dog they were talking about.

"Astra!" I pushed my way through the crowd. Akiko, Mae, and Hopscotch raced close behind me. What would Mrs. B do without her loyal sidekick? Even though their powers had been drained, they would always be superheroes to me. And I knew Akiko and Mae felt the same way.

"Side-Splitter's pull," Mrs. B said, her voice weak. "It

sapped everything from us. But poor Astra, it's as if he has nothing left."

"The Infinity Trinity put a stop to Side-Splitter," Hopscotch told her, placing a reassuring hand on Mrs. B's shoulder. "He won't hurt anyone else again."

Astra looked almost puppyish as he lay curled up on the cable car's wooden floor. His eyes were open, but he didn't have the energy to even lift his head. It was all I could do not to cry.

"Astra," I whispered, my lips near his ear. I wrapped my arms around him and pressed my forehead to his. With all my might, I concentrated. I thought about the good things he and Mrs. B had done as Star and the Palomino. I thought of the way they'd pushed back against evil villains, protected people in danger, and rescued animals and others from harm. Astra was the smartest dog I'd ever met. And one of the kindest creatures to ever place four paws on the earth.

Squeezing my eyes tight, I thought of all the people who loved him.

Akiko stepped in close and laid her hands on his side. Mae joined her.

"His tail," hollered someone in the crowd. "It's wagging!"

"Astra's feeling better, Emerald Shield," Akiko said, giving my arm a squeeze. Her voice snapped me back to the moment. It was like waking from a dream. My hands were hot, and I felt beads of sweat at my forehead and under my mask.

"And what he really wants," added Mae, gently rubbing his forehead, "is a slice of pie."

"Me too," I whispered. "And a cold milkshake."

Mrs. B let out a sigh of relief and leaned against the cable car beside Astra. She held Akiko's hand and gave us each a grateful smile. She seemed to have aged a hundred years today. I wanted to heal her, too—wanted to stop this terrible force that was draining the life right out of them.

Mae gasped. "Orange Inferno, didn't we find something today that might help? Remember? The Emerald Shield snatched them back, and we saved them in your bag!"

Mae was right. How could we have forgotten? When we'd caught the Doll Lady passing on the moonstone collar and ring, we'd recognized them right away as belonging to Star and the Palomino.

"Here, if you had part of your costumes," Akiko said softly, reaching into the pouch at her waist, "then maybe you'd find your strength again."

When she opened her hand, the moonstone ring was sitting in her palm and pulsing like a firefly. Mrs. B's eyes grew wide, and I could tell she was surprised. I wondered how long it had been since she and Astra had been able to transform into the Palomino and Star and fly together as superheroes.

She carefully slid her ring onto the middle finger of her right hand. And as if a light switch flipped, Mrs. B seemed to radiate back to life. The gray pallor of her skin gave way to a healthy glow, and her eyes lit up brighter than I'd seen since arriving in San Francisco.

"What about the collar?" she asked, her voice sounding hopeful. She got to her feet, stiffness dropping from her shoulders like an old shawl.

Akiko reached into her pouch again. And then she knelt down and fastened the collar around Astra's neck. He lifted his nose to the wind and sniffed in all directions. Then he rose to his feet and shook his body from ears to tail, as if he'd just come in from the rain.

When Astra bounded off the cable car in a graceful leap, the crowd erupted in a noisy cheer. It startled the birds perched on rooftops and telephone wires all around us. Shouts and hollers took wing with the pigeons and gulls and pelicans as the whole waterfront seemed to celebrate.

Even the police were buoyant as they carted off wagon after wagon filled with Side-Splitter's army of clowns. "That's the end of this bad guy. Thank goodness for those superkids," an officer was saying to his partner as they dragged a woozy Side-Splitter into the police wagon. A third officer walked behind them, and I noticed he was carrying a bowler hat and a buzzer ring. "This guy was serious trouble."

"They caught some spy, too," said the partner, nodding toward another black-and-white police wagon. "Something to do with dolls or toys. This world keeps getting stranger and stranger."

I could see a bright pink hat through the rear window of the wagon as it passed, sirens blaring. I wondered if Akiko did too. But before I had a chance to speak, Mrs. B and Astra headed off in the opposite direction, slipping away before they drew any more attention to themselves. It occurred to me that maybe Akiko, Mae, and I should do the same.

"Well done, Infinity Trinity," called Hopscotch with a ghostly wave as her scooter zipped away. "Hauntima was right—you are our hope!"

My heart swelled in my chest. Hopscotch thought we'd done all right? And Hauntima, too? I wanted to chase after her and ask her to stay.

"Don't they remind you of somebody we used to know?" asked a woman bouncing a baby on her hip. Her eyes were on Mrs. B and Astra, who were already halfway down the street.

"I got the strangest feeling," answered the man beside her. "An old memory played in my mind like a movie reel. I was thinking about the superheroes I adored back when I was a kid. Remember them? Hopscotch, Hauntima, Nova the Sunchaser. And especially the Palomino and her sidekick—what was his name?"

The woman nodded excitedly. "It was Star! He was a wolf-hero!"

"That's right," said the man, staring after Mrs. B and Astra. "It's the darnedest thing. I haven't thought of them in years."

"The Palomino had a powerful sister, too," said the woman, shifting the baby to her other hip. "She also wore the moonstone. She was Zena . . . no, Zania . . ."

"Zenobia," Akiko reminded them. "They were some of the greats. But they're not gone forever. They'll be back."

Mae and I joined with her. "We promise."

Thirty-Nine

$\mathcal{W}$E WERE BACK AT ROOM TWELVE IN THE blink of an eye.

I wasn't exactly exaggerating, either. Grabbing hands and teleporting with Akiko's help really *did* happen in the blink of an eye. And transforming from our superhero costumes into our everyday clothes took only seconds too.

"Are you happy now, Akiko?" teased Mae as we caught our breath. Instead of teleporting onto the roof again, Akiko had taken us directly to Room Twelve. "With that gadget bag, you've got another superpower. Which means you have one more than Josie and me."

Akiko grinned and patted the familiar canvas pouch

hanging across her chest. While it came in handy for the ordinary, day-to-day demands of being a kid, it was pretty amazing for the extraordinary needs of battling supervillains. I tried to tamp down a pang of jealousy over Akiko having more powers than we did. Instead I focused on the fact that her bag helped us all defeat Side-Splitter.

She pulled out gum and passed us each a piece.

"Side-Splitter's heading to prison," she said as we opened the door from the small gym and into the bustling office. "Thanks to us, the city, the bridges, and the ships are safe. And those secret messages transmitted to the enemy have been cut off, for now."

"And all those clowns who were willing to carry out Side-Splitter's evil deeds," I said with a shudder, "thank goodness they're done for too."

Room Twelve was humming with activity, and a fluffy ball of brown-and-white fur bounded over to us. "Astra!" squealed Mae, dropping to her knees and hugging our four-legged friend. "It's so good to see you feeling yourself again!"

Akiko and I squatted down beside Astra and gave his ears, back, and belly a good scratching. His tail was a windshield wiper on the fastest setting, which made me laugh out loud.

Ah-choo!

Akiko still had her allergies. But that didn't stop her from planting a kiss on Astra's head.

"What a relief to see him back to his old self," I said. "I

can't believe how close Side-Splitter came to doing him in. And Mrs. B, too."

Akiko's face turned serious. "He's not the only one to be locked up. The Doll Lady," she said, hesitating, "she's going behind bars too. But what I still can't understand is—"

"Your mom," interrupted Mae.

"Right," Akiko said sadly, staring into Astra's eyes. "I guess she got caught up with bad people. Whether they were forcing her or . . . I still don't understand what made her want to help the Doll Lady."

Mae made a little *ahem* noise. Then she started again, pointing toward the doorway behind Akiko and me.

"No, I mean, your mom, Akiko. She's here! In Room Twelve!"

Akiko looked up. The red door leading to the radio room was open, and just inside stood a woman we'd only glimpsed from a distance. On her head was the familiar green beret, but now she was pressing a radio headset to one of her ears. She was deep in discussion with Genevieve and Elizebeth.

Akiko bolted across the room and flung her arms around the woman's neck. "Mom," she said, seeming to exhale the word rather than speak it. "You're okay!"

All the worry of the past few days melted away as they stood there hugging.

"Akiko!" her mom exclaimed. She stepped back to study

her daughter's face. "I cannot believe it's you! How? Why? What are you doing here?"

"I want to know the same thing about you," gushed Akiko. "Did anyone hurt you? What have you been doing? How did you get involved in this?"

Mrs. B joined us in the doorway.

"As you know by now," she began, "the extraordinary can be found amid the ordinary. It's just a matter of adjusting the way we look at things."

Akiko kept staring into her mom's face, glancing quickly at Mrs. B and then back.

"Your mother, Akiko," Mrs. B went on, "is one of thousands—make that hundreds of thousands—of women helping in our battle to win the war. We know our men are sacrificing their lives fighting on land, by air, and by sea. But our women are doing remarkable things too—as you know from your introduction to Noor Khan, Genevieve Grotjan, and Elizebeth Friedman.

"Our Japanese American sisters are no less brave, volunteering to help as linguists, in cryptography, in communications, as translators. Many have even joined the war effort straight from internment camps."

Akiko looked like she needed a chair. Astra nudged one with his nose, and Mae scooted it closer. I helped Akiko sit down, and Mae quickly pulled over a chair for Akiko's mom to take too.

"But the Doll Lady," Akiko croaked. "We saw you with her, spying on those ships along the waterfront. You were passing information on to Side-Splitter, to the enemy. It was your old saying—the one about *raining gnats and frogs!*"

Before Akiko's mom could speak, Mrs. B explained. "The key element of our league of secret heroes is just that: *secret.*" She paused, watching Akiko's face closely. "For our very survival, it is crucial that we protect each and every member's identity. This is why we did not tell either of you about the other. I hope you will understand."

Extraordinary amid the ordinary. I liked the idea of that. But sometimes the extraordinary could bowl you over like a hurricane. I looked over at Mae. Tapping my finger to my chin, I signaled for her to close her jaw. It was hanging open like a broken drawer.

"So my mom isn't . . . ," Akiko began, looking up at Mrs. B and shrugging. "She's not—"

Akiko was so thrown off, she kept interrupting herself.

"My mom isn't a spy? She's been helping Room Twelve too?"

Mrs. B beamed at her.

As the realization finally hit, Akiko beamed right back.

"And you, Akiko?" said her mom, who all of a sudden looked like a worried parent rather than a secret operative. "You aren't skipping school, are you? Or avoiding hard work at your aunt and uncle's store?"

Akiko denied anything to do with skipping school or avoiding work, and Mae and I joined in to help defend her. "We're good at puzzles, Mom," she said, pointing in our direction. "These are my friends, Mae and Josie. The three of us, we've done our best for Room Twelve too. And we—"

And her thoughts seemed to get tangled up in a jumble of explanations. How much should she reveal? Was it okay to tell her mom about the code cracking? What about the Infinity Trinity? And the Orange Inferno? With the power to fly and shape-shift and shoot fireballs?

I thought about my own mom. She believed I was at summer camp. And so did Granny Crumpler. The fewer people who knew our secret identities, the better.

"Actually, we . . we're . . . ," started Mae, trying to help out.

Thankfully, Mrs. B stepped in.

"We have been lucky to have their help. Akiko, Josie, and Mae have proven themselves to be exceptional puzzlers," she said. "Room Twelve is deeply grateful."

Just then a commotion went up at the back of the radio room, and someone urgently signaled for Akiko's mother to join in.

Mae and I watched Akiko's expression as they hugged goodbye.

"It's good to know you're still just my mom," Akiko said, squeezing her eyes shut and resting her chin on her mother's shoulder. "Although you're so much more than a regular old mom—extraordinary amid the ordinary."

"And you, Akiko," she replied, giving one last squeeze to Akiko's shoulders. "Solving puzzles is a real skill—a power. You and your friends can pretend you're caped heroes, just like the ones you love in those comic books!"

Akiko's eyes flew open.

She began to sputter and cough. Thankfully, as Mae and I rushed to her side, Akiko's mom dashed off into the radio room and shut the red door.

"Well," Mae said with a friendly pat on Akiko's back, "I don't think your mom knows about the Infinity Trinity."

"Or if she does"—I laughed—"she doesn't know we're it!"

Suddenly Mrs. B's assistants arrived, placing three slices of pie and three milkshakes at the table. On the floor beside us, they set a special bowl for Astra: his very own slice of pie, though from the look of it, there might have been dog chow in there instead of gooey, warm fruit.

My stomach growled at the sight and smell of my all-time favorite meal: blueberry pie and a brown cow. For Akiko, a slice of apple pie and an egg cream. And for Mae, cherry pie and a chocolate malted. We slid into our chairs and got busy, issuing a few thank-yous in between bites and slurps.

Even Astra seemed excited as he wolfed down his dessert. Once he finished, he jumped onto the brown steamer trunk to sit near us.

"As we learned from our work with Agent Khan," Mrs. B said, reaching over to a desk where an assistant had just set down the afternoon newspapers, "women make good spies because society doesn't expect women to be so bold. It's simply a lack of imagination, really. History for too long has taught that females are delicate flowers, unable to take the heat, incapable of feats of strength and daring."

Unfolding a front page, she pointed to a photo of the Infinity Trinity splashed across it.

"But we know better."

Forty

SUDDENLY THE DOOR TO THE RADIO ROOM opened again, and Genevieve appeared. She rushed to Mrs. B with a notebook clutched to her chest.

"We've picked up another transmission," she said. Elizebeth and Agent Khan followed close behind her. "This one is as faint as the others. I worry that we might lose them entirely."

"I fear the same," Mrs. B said. Her eyes raced across Genevieve's paper. Then she turned the page toward us. "It's crucial that we solve this as quickly as we can. So many lives are in danger."

Her voice was tight, and I knew she must have been thinking about Zenobia.

"We'll give it a good shot," said Akiko, grabbing a stack of paper and three pencils. "Is it another grid? An acrostic? A substitution code?"

The three of us fell silent as we wrote down what Genevieve's paper showed us:

IF ELF WERE TO
SHINE GLOOP

"Gloop?" I exclaimed. "Looks as if we unscramble it."

"This is an easy one!" said Akiko, breathing fast as her pencil scratched across the paper.

"There are a lot of *F*s," said Mae, just as breathless. "Think of words with repeated *F*s in them!"

We wrote down everything that came to mind, comparing pages as we went. My pencil seemed to fly as I scribbled down *effect, affect, effort*. Mae and Akiko had *coffee, toffee, spiffy, buff, stuff, huff*. But then it hit me. In one of the messages we'd cracked before, there was an S-O-S call that said something about Nazis and a tower.

"Eiffel," I said, nearly shouting. "There was a clue earlier about a tower. That first line could be about the Eiffel Tower!"

Mae nodded as she ticked off the letters. Her face was as tense as I'd ever seen it. "You're right, Josie. We talked about Paris before. I think the messenger could be transmitting from there."

"We are treating this as a Code Red emergency," added Elizebeth, pacing beside us. "There is a great deal at stake."

We raced to unscramble the second line. What in the world could SHINE GLOOP possibly stand for? Mae was muttering possibilities under her breath, and Akiko was practically panting. Then, at the same time, they began hollering words they formed from the letters.

"Long ship!" called one.

"Poison!" shouted the other.

We fell silent, staring at the message and willing it to reveal its secret to us. I could see those words in the scramble. But after I ticked off each letter, the ones left over made no sense. Astra barked, circling the lid of the steamer trunk and urging us on.

Finally, Mae hit on something.

"Losing," she said.

"Hope," added Akiko right behind her, voice catching in her throat.

The room fell quiet as we stared at each other. On my paper, I ticked off the letters for every word again, checking their work. Akiko and Mae were right. There were no extra letters. I wrote out the message.

EIFFEL TOWER
LOSING HOPE

Mrs. B picked up my paper and walked to the other side of the room. I heard her take a deep breath as she stared at the page.

I had seen enough postcards and news reels at the movie theaters to know what the Eiffel Tower looked like. Whenever someone mentioned France, it was the image that popped into my head: a towering iron structure criss-crossed like a garden lattice and soaring into the sky. I knew the Nazi flag was hanging there now. I wondered how the French people felt about that. How would we feel if the Nazi banner hung from our Statue of Liberty?

"The Eiffel Tower was built in 1889 for the World's Fair," announced Akiko.

"And it's as tall as an eighty-story building," added Mae.

Mrs. B turned around, squaring her shoulders as she looked at us. I expected tears to be filling her eyes. But instead she studied our faces with a ferocity that made me jump.

"Now it is abundantly clear," she began. "We know where we need to focus our attention, our resources, and our energy. There are many brave souls facing desperate odds who need our help."

She paused, gazing back down at the message.

"The answer to one of the biggest questions that Room Twelve has been puzzling over is the Eiffel Tower in Paris, France."

"I'll be there soon," whispered Agent Khan. "Transmitting from Paris is riskier than ever."

Mae cleared her throat. She raised one hand slightly, as if she were in a classroom and not the headquarters of the league of secret heroes. "So this message," she began politely, "it tells us *where* the call for help is coming from. But there's another question, and that's—"

"Who," interrupted Akiko. "*Who* is sending the call? That's something we don't know."

Mrs. B tapped her leg, summoning Astra to her side. He hopped off the brown steamer trunk and crossed the room to stand next to her. Thankfully, they looked stronger than they had in days. Though his brown-and-white fur hid part of his collar, I could see the moonstone there, shining brightly.

"Unfortunately, we do," she said. "And it's time we let you know too."

Elizebeth, Genevieve, and Agent Khan excused themselves and took this latest message back to the radio room to share with the others. Hurrying through the red door, they looked as if they were eager to return to their radios and headsets. As the door clicked shut, Mrs. B turned to us and spoke in a low voice.

"The three of you have figured out so many puzzles already in your short time with Room Twelve," she began. "You deciphered who I am. You deduced who Astra is too. And you solved the riddle of my missing sister.

"Zenobia means the world to me."

She paused, and a sob swept over me like an ocean wave. I thought of my father and how much I missed him. I sneaked a look at Mae and knew she was thinking of her dad too, risking his life in France. And I could see Akiko fiddling with her bag. Her brother, Tommy, was never far from her thoughts. All of us had people who meant the world to us.

Mrs. B stepped over to the steamer trunk and ran her hands over a lock. She turned the brass dials and aligned a row of numbers and symbols. Then, with a click, the trunk's ancient-looking lid popped open about an inch.

As Mrs. B lifted it all the way up, I felt the energy in the room quicken. A faint buzzing, like a swarm of bees, filled my ears. I turned to Akiko, knowing that if this were an earthquake, she'd tell us. But she and Mae were silent and focused as the three of us pressed close together at the trunk's edge.

We leaned forward and peered inside.

"Costumes?" croaked Akiko. "Is that what's in here?"

"I see boots," Mae said slowly. "Lots of them. And capes. And those are—"

"Masks," interrupted Akiko. "That red one looks like it belongs to the Ruby Hummingbird. She went missing years ago, at the start of the war."

My mouth went dry. I knew if I tried to speak, no words would come out.

I stared at the trunk's contents and tried to make sense of what I was seeing. Bright blues and greens, shiny reds and oranges, glimmering purples and yellows. And there, off to the right, I saw black. I started to reach for it—I could tell it was a cape—but as my fingers came close to the shimmering fabric, a charge surged through me. I yanked my hand back, fingers tingling.

"Th-that black cape," I managed. "I know that cape. It was the Stretcher's, wasn't it?"

"When the three of you first encountered what was left of the Stretcher's costume—his cape, mask, and boots—there was still a force empowering it," Mrs. B explained. "I believe that's what helped to bring out your own powers. And, of course, you did the rest."

The terrible image of the Stretcher being vaporized played in my head. I squeezed my eyes shut, trying to forget the awful scene.

"My sister has gone missing," Mrs. B said, twisting the moonstone ring on her finger, "and as we battle with the vast forces of evil in the world, I am more determined than ever to bring her back."

I could see Mae and Akiko nodding enthusiastically, and I felt the same way. We all wanted to rescue Zenobia and see her return to fighting evil. But I still couldn't believe that the league of secret heroes thought we were the ones who could do it.

Three kids?

To help save the most remarkable superhero of all time?

"But Zenobia is not alone," Mrs. B continued. "Far too many of our finest have disappeared. I regret that you had to witness the destruction of the Stretcher. And you are already aware of the struggle Hauntima and Hopscotch have faced to use what remains of their powers. They are mere ghosts of what they once were."

I couldn't help but stare at Mrs. B and Astra, studying their faces and their forms.

"And what about you?" I asked. "Why can't you transform back into the Palomino and Star?"

Mae was the one who spotted it. She reached into the trunk and unfurled a shimmering golden cape. Embroidered in the center was the red silhouette of a proud horse. Akiko pulled out a smaller golden cape. When she shook it out, we saw a red star. They were the costumes for the Palomino and Star! It had been ages since I'd seen them in action!

"They tried to stop us," Mrs. B said, and a cloud passed behind her eyes. "They nearly did. Their attacks took away much of our power, but it could never destroy our spirit. That is something I believe will always live on."

Akiko reached over to Astra and scratched his fur.

"But Astra's moonstone collar and your moonstone ring," she said. "They still give you some amount of power, right?"

Mrs. B nodded. "Thanks to you, we have the moon-stones once again. Their powers somehow combat the evil force that's being used to drain superheroes. Therefore, Astra and I will be able to keep on fighting, though we'll continue to use means other than traditional superpowers."

I knew she meant Room Twelve.

"But what about Zenobia?" I asked. "She wore a moon-stone ring too, right? Your mother, the Masked Moon-flower, gave them to you when you were kids."

But before Mrs. B could answer, Mae reached her hand into the trunk.

"No!" She gasped. In her hand sat a ring bearing a round white stone. "This must be Zenobia's moonstone. If it's not on her finger like yours, that means she's—"

"Powerless," I said, the puzzle pieces finally clicking together. "That was the word in the message! Zenobia is at the Eiffel Tower. She's the one transmitting the messages calling for help. She's the one we need to go to Paris for and bring back home."

I expected Mrs. B to agree, maybe even offer us an encouraging word. But instead she just shook her head.

"Not only Zenobia," she whispered. And I saw her eyes flash as she scanned the trunk full of capes, masks, and boots that had once belonged to so many other superheroes.

"All of them. Bring them all back."

AUTHOR'S NOTE

$\mathcal{H}$ISTORY TELLS US WHERE WE CAME FROM and shapes what we'll be. In researching the League of Secret Heroes series, I found it fascinating that the popularity of comic book superheroes ran parallel with World War II history. I became interested in ideas of power and powerlessness—not just in terms of caped heroes, but of everyday people too. As I wrote *Mask*, I wondered if it was possible that America could ever again violate the rights of its citizens on a scale as big as what was done to Japanese Americans during the war.

In 1941, when America was attacked by the Japanese military at Pearl Harbor and entered WWII, people suddenly turned on Japanese Americans. Within months, the government was rounding up families on the West Coast and forcing them into camps in the desert, fearing they might be spies or saboteurs. From babies all the way up to grandparents, Japanese American citizens and Japanese immigrants had to leave their homes to live in internment camps for the duration of the war, which lasted until 1945.

The government eventually issued an apology for its actions, after it was found that the decision to imprison Japanese Americans was based on "race prejudice, war hysteria, and a failure of political leadership." But nothing could ever give the years back to those who were locked up. When the war ended and the camps closed down, Japanese Americans were issued twenty-five dollars and a train or bus ticket to start their lives over. That hardly covered all that they'd lost.

To learn more about WWII experiences, we don't have to rely only on books. We just have to reach out and listen to one another's stories. Some internment camp survivors are still living. For others, their children keep their stories alive. When I interviewed one survivor, she told me what it was like as a girl to be sent from her home in California to Arkansas's Jerome and Rohwer War Relocation Centers. "We had two dogs, and they were poisoned. They weren't Japanese. They were dogs. Who would do that? My parents must have felt terrible," she said. "I think the camp days made me stronger and tougher in accepting life as it is—in trying to make the best of it. We all choose different ways in going through life. I saw the ways my parents tried to go through it with dignity and trying to protect us."

A daughter of another survivor told me about her mom, who was interned at the Minidoka War Relocation Center in Idaho. She had saved thick scrapbooks and yearbooks filled with programs, letters, and notes documenting her time there as a girl. She was clearly a big personality—voted "Cutest in Class"—and aside from writing poetry, she wrote her own sick notes to get out of school.

There are other interesting windows into history throughout *Mask*. What follows are some of the facts amid the fiction:

Japanese Balloon Bomb

In the book, we see supervillain Side-Splitter summoning balloon bombs. But a little-known part of history is that, during the war, Japan sent deadly balloons riding the air stream across the Pacific Ocean to bomb American cities, farms, and forests—setting fires and causing panic. Each balloon was about thirty feet in diameter, and dangling from it were bombs that featured trigger devices and explosive powder. An estimated one thousand of them made it all the way to North America, according to *National Geographic*, but just under three hundred have been recorded. On May 5, 1945, an American woman and five children were killed after they discovered a large paper balloon during a picnic in the woods of Bly, Oregon. Theirs were the only deaths caused by enemy attack on the American mainland during WWII.

"I Am an American" Sign

Photograph by Dorothea Lange, March 1942
Photo courtesy of the Library of Congress

While the story of Akiko and her mom is fictional, after the bombing of Pearl Harbor in December 1941, Japanese

Americans were suddenly called "an enemy race," regardless of how many generations they'd been living as citizens of the United States. I placed the iconic "I Am an American" image on Akiko's old street in Japantown, a neighborhood in San Francisco, but the real sign was put up at the grocery store owned by the Matsuda family in Oakland, California, just across the Bay.

Executive Order 9066

President Franklin Delano Roosevelt signed the order on February 19, 1942, which authorized forcing about 120,000 people of Japanese descent from their homes along the West Coast and into any of ten internment camps (also called concentration camps), like Manzanar in the California desert, because of their ethnic background. The majority of those evacuated were born in America. This order is considered one of the worst violations of Americans' civil rights in the twentieth century.

The 442nd Regimental Combat Team

I wanted to write about Akiko's brother, Tommy, belonging to the US Army's 442nd Regimental Combat Team because it is the most highly decorated military unit in American history. Composed almost entirely of Japanese American soldiers, many of whom signed up to serve America while imprisoned in the camps, the regiment fought in Italy, France, and Germany. With a motto of "Go for Broke," they were sent into some of the most intense battles of the war. The men serving in the 442nd were awarded over 18,000 honors, including 9,486 Purple Hearts and 5,200 Bronze Star medals, 21 Medal of Honor awards, the Congressional Gold Medal, as well as being honored by the French Légion d'Honneur. Visit the Go for Broke National Education Center to learn more about the 442nd Regimental Combat Team at GoforBroke.org.

Genevieve Grotjan and Elizebeth Friedman

Genevieve Grotjan (left) and Elizebeth Friedman
Photo courtesy of the National Security Agency, NSA.gov

Elizebeth Friedman is considered the first-ever female cryptologist. Her love of puzzles and ciphers led her into a career as a government code breaker and demonstrated the importance of code breaking and deciphering in crime prevention. During the Prohibition era in the 1920s, when alcohol was illegal, she solved tens of thousands of messages involving smuggling. Elizebeth went on to work on the Doll Lady case of Velvalee Dickinson and then to solving encoded messages Nazi Germany was sending on their cipher machine, called Enigma. Because J. Edgar Hoover, head of the Federal Bureau of Investigation (FBI), took credit for Elizebeth's and her team's accomplishments, her tremendous contribution to cryptology was not well-known until after her death. In 2002, the National Security Agency named its auditorium the William F. Friedman and Elizebeth S. Friedman Memorial Auditorium. Learn more about Elizebeth at the National Security Agency's website at NSA.gov.

Mathematician Genevieve Grotjan worked for the Signal Intelligence Service under William Friedman, husband of Elizebeth Friedman and himself a brilliant code cracker. Like the Germans with their Enigma machine, Japan's military used a cipher machine they called Purple and transmitted their encoded messages over the radio. A US radio station would intercept the Japanese messages and send them on to offices in Washington for code crackers to try to decipher. Genevieve's breakthrough in cracking

Purple has been called, in the *Encyclopedia of American Women at War*, "one of the greatest achievements in the history of US code breaking." The US Navy suddenly had a window into what the Japanese military was plotting and could plan for attacks by air, land, and sea accordingly. Read more about Genevieve's real-life code-cracking moments at NSA.gov.

How did the team celebrate Genevieve cracking Purple? According to historians, they sent out for bottles of Coca-Cola!

The Doll Lady

Velvalee Dickinson, nicknamed the "Doll Lady" or the "Doll Woman," ran a doll store in New York that also sold antiques and toys. For *Mask*, I moved her shop to San Francisco. She and her husband took spying trips to the West Coast to record what they saw at naval shipyards in San Francisco and San

Diego and pass along information about warships to Japan. Her spying letters were sent through a contact in South America, but some were marked undeliverable and returned to the United States, which caught the attention of the FBI. In chapter twenty-four, a real example of the Doll Lady's cryptic letters is given. Elizebeth Friedman was already legendary as a code cracker when she was called upon to help solve the Doll Lady case. Velvalee was found guilty in 1944 and sent to prison for ten years. Read more about her at FBI.gov.

Noor Khan

Noor Inayat Khan, a British secret agent of Indian Muslim and American descent, was the first female radio operator sent into Nazi-occupied France by the British spy agency SOE (Special Operations Executive). A writer of children's books and poetry before the war broke out, Noor wanted to do her part to defeat the Nazis. She trained

Photo courtesy of the Imperial War Museums

as a spy and learned to send and receive crucial messages about sabotage, weapons, and the needs of France's resistance fighters. I share a powerful direct quote from Noor about the dangers of her spy mission in chapter twenty-six: "I know I risk my life, since that is how most people end who do this work." She was Britain's first Muslim war heroine, and a statue stands in London to honor her service. Learn more about Noor at BBC.com.

ACKNOWLEDGMENTS

$\mathcal{G}$RATEFUL THANKS TO JEAN MISHIMA, president of the Chicago Japanese American Historical Society (CJAHS) and also an internee at the Gila River War Relocation Center in Arizona, for a thoughtful reading of my manuscript and lending insights and understanding to how Akiko's story was presented. To learn more about Japanese Americans and internment camp experiences, visit CJAHS.org as well as the National Archives at www.archives.gov/education/lessons/Japanese-relocation.

Thanks also to family friend Suzy Nakamura for sharing with me the scrapbooks and stories of her mother, Sada Yasuda, who had been imprisoned at the Minidoka War Relocation Center in southern Idaho; fellow Chicagoan Keith Uchima for talking to me about his mother, Ruth Chiyoko Yoshida-Uchima, and writing about her time imprisoned at Manzanar War Relocation Center in California; and Takayo (Tsubouchi) Fischer for speaking to me about her personal experiences during and immediately after WWII and her time at the Jerome and Rohwer War Relocation Centers in Arkansas.